The Ride

BY

JUSTIN REICHMAN

For information about Scobre...

Scobre Press Corporation
2255 Calle Clara
La Jolla, CA 92037

Scobre Press books may be purchased for educational, business or sales promotional use.

Edited by Helen Glenn Court
Illustrated by Gail Piazza
Cover Design by Michael Lynch

ISBN 1-933423-25-0

HOME RUN EDITION

www.scobre.com

CHAPTER ONE

BIG CHILL

I was in the gate with two minutes remaining before the last heat of the day. I guess I should have been nervous, but I wasn't. I was more excited than anything. I was standing at the top of the Big Chill. More people got injured on the Big Chill than any other run in Wyoming. I think it's because they don't know the run. I've ridden the Big Chill so many times I could do it with my eyes closed. Not that I would ever snowboard with my eyes closed.

"Thirty seconds," the race official called out.

I quickly double checked my binding, making sure it was tight. Then I pulled my goggles over my helmet. I was ready. I was psyched.

"Ten seconds."

I began to rock my board back and forth. My snowboard slid easily across the snow. I took one final, excited, deep breath. Then I blew out hard, puffing my cheeks.

"Five, four, three, two, one, go!" The gun sounded.

I flew out of the gate the instant it opened. The first part of the run was a narrow chute. All I could do was tuck, pick up speed, and not fall down. After a few seconds, the slope became a bit less steep. Although I was moving at a good speed, I had a second to look around. There wasn't much to see. The trees and rocks were a total blur. I smiled from ear to ear.

We had gotten fresh snow the night before so my board sunk down into the powder. I leaned back to spread my weight across the snow. I knew I was fine when I saw snow spray from my board. A thin mist of powder hit my face. At that moment, I was sure that I was winning.

I fought through the powder. I turned only when I absolutely had to. Otherwise, I kept my line straight down the course. I was really moving. Not out of control, though. I'm never out of control—especially on the Big Chill.

The course opened up into a mogul field. A mogul is a big hard mound of snow on a run. It's not a jump—it's more of an obstacle. If you hit a mogul the wrong way, you'll land face first. If you face plant when you're going as fast as I go, it really hurts. I knew every bump on the run, though. There was no way I would hit one wrong.

I moved through the mogul field with ease. I got a little bit of air a couple of times, but nothing too big. This was all about speed. I took each bump exactly as planned.

After I passed through the mogul field, there was a final jump before the finish. It wasn't much. But when you're going fast, even a little jump can turn into big air. I tucked down low and really went for it. I wanted this to be the best run of the day. Not just my best run, but *the* best run.

My board lifted off the ground and I felt as if I were flying. I grabbed my board with both hands. I could see the finish in front of me. There was a small crowd that had gathered. I tried not to look at them. From the corner of my eye, though, something seemed out of the ordinary. I barely turned my head, wondering: is that a gorilla wearing a clown wig?

Just like that, it was over. I lost control for a second—a split second. My balance shifted. Not too much, but just enough to mess up my landing. The first thing to hit the snow was the front edge of my board. I was moving forward at full speed, so when I hit the ground, I hit hard. My board dug deep into the snow and stopped when it hit the frozen surface. My body, of course, shot forward. I hit the packed snow ten feet in front of where my board landed. I hit hard, with a loud thud that I could hear and feel in my ears. Instantly, the breath was knocked from my lungs. My teeth rattled inside my head.

Everything became a blur. My mouth and nose filled with snow. My goggles flew off my helmet. I opened and closed my eyes as I flipped down the hill. I caught a glimpse of the sky, then some snow. This cycle repeated itself as I kept flipping—sky, snow, sky, snow. I felt like I was caught in a washing machine. I tried to stop, but there was nothing I could do.

I ended up flat on my back, sliding down the hill. When I opened my eyes, I saw that I had rolled past the finish line. I leaned up and looked at the crowd staring down at me on the ground. Mixed in the group of people was someone in a gorilla suit and a clown wig. What was that guy thinking?

I squinted to read the bib the person was wearing on his gorilla chest. It read, "I go ape for Mad Marty in the Mornings on 104.5." As I finished reading, I realized who was inside the gorilla suit. It was my father—Mad Marty Morgan.

There might have been a time when I was more upset with my dad. But at that moment, I couldn't remember it. I sat up, stretching my body to make sure I hadn't broken any bones. Then I got to my feet. That was when I began planning how I was going to move out of my house. I would go live with my best friend Sally—away from my embarrassing father.

Just then, a voice rang out over the loudspeakers. "Despite her odd finish, Cece Morgan grabs first place in the thirteen-and-under girls' category." This announcement was followed by some applause from the crowd. I gave a wave. The voice went on, "the final results are now in. The overall winner of the Rockville Junior Snowboard Jam is. . . " I took a deep breath. ". . . Chad Doogan." I let out a sigh.

My name is Cece Morgan, not Chad Doogan. I know Chad Doogan, and he's a jerk. I undid my binding and walked away from the crowd. At least I wasn't injured from my big wipeout, which I guess was lucky. At the moment, though, I didn't feel very lucky. I thought I might just be the unluckiest person on the planet. How many other kids had a gorilla for a father?

I walked over to the tent where they posted the day's results. It was true. Chad Doogan, the biggest jerk in Rockville, had beaten me by 3.2 seconds. 3.2 seconds!

That wipeout cost me the championship. I felt like punching something. I felt like crying. I felt like screaming at the top of my lungs. I felt a tap on my shoulder. I turned around. There was no one there. I felt a tap on my other shoulder. I turned around again. There was still no one there. I knew only one person who was childish enough to think that this was funny. I stared straight ahead. "Stop it, Dad."

"Congratulations, Chili," my father said through his gorilla suit. I ignored him. I crossed my arms tight across my chest. "Come on, Chili, you won your age group. That's fantastic!"

He didn't get it. Winning my age group wasn't enough. Today was supposed to be my day! I was *supposed* to win the whole thing! The reason I didn't win was because of him. He just didn't get it.

I finally turned around. It was worse than I imagined. Not only was my dad a gorilla, he was also a clown. He was wearing a full gorilla suit. On top of his mask sat a big rainbow colored wig. He wore ridiculously large sunglasses too. A big red clown nose hung from his face. He was also wearing rainbow suspenders and a yellow bow tie. And, oh yeah, a giant diaper.

"Dad, please walk away from me. Pretend we don't know each other."

"What's wrong, Chili?" he asked, pulling his mask off. His light brown and gray hair stuck straight up.

"Dad, I never would have wiped out if you weren't wearing that stupid costume. You made me blow my concentration! And if I didn't crash, I would have won. I would have beaten Chad Doogan."

My dad stared at me, silent for a moment. "Beaten Doogan, huh?"

I nodded.

"Chili, I'm sorry." He hung his head. "I just came to see you race. I would never do anything to mess you up. Today is such a crowded day, I thought I'd advertise for the show." He stared down at the snow again, then back up at me. "Honey, you were great!"

When Dad looked at me like that, it was impossible to stay mad at him. So instead, I just smiled. "Let's go, Dad. You're such a goofball." I grabbed his arm and we made our way toward the parking lot. I knew he didn't mean to ruin my concentration. He really is a great person. He's just kind of weird too.

Before we stepped into the parking lot, Chad Doogan walked up to me. "Great race, Cece. I was worried there for a second. Lucky for me that jump got you at the end. Now *that's* drama." He smiled his confident smile. I wanted to tackle him. "Better luck next year," he said. He turned to face my dad. "Hey, Mr. Morgan. Love the outfit." He laughed and walked away.

CHAPTER TWO

GROWING UP CHILI

My name is Cece, but my dad calls me Chili. I'm not exactly sure why, but he's called me that since I was a kid. I'm twelve now and I'm in sixth grade. I guess I'm about average height, with long brown hair. People say I have a pretty face. But people used to think the world was flat, too—and you know how that theory turned out.

Anyway, my whole life I've lived in Rockville, Wyoming—population 6,537. I've watched enough television to know that I live in a very small town. Downtown Rockville is just a single block long. There's Pick 'n Save Grocery store, two banks, Rockville Public Library and Wendell's Drug Store. Don't forget the Rockville Hardware, Rockville Post Office, Clean as a Whistle Dry Cleaners, Tony and Terry's Pizza and Pasta. That's it and that's all. If you need some clothes, you have to drive thirty minutes to Jackson Hole.

But there is one thing we have that is bigger and better than anywhere else. We have the best, most beautiful mountain to snowboard on. Snowboarding, by the way, is my favorite thing in the world to do. *Snowboarding Times* called Rockville Mountain one of the best-kept secrets in the USA. When that article came out, I remembered hoping that nobody outside of Rockville read it. The last thing we need is lots of tourists slowing up our mountain.

From my front door, I can be up on the mountain in fourteen minutes. There's enough snow to snowboard from October to April. So, for six months of the year, I am as far from being bored as possible. I snowboard on weekend days and at least three days during the week.

When vacations come around, I don't like to go anywhere. I stay home and snowboard. I'm good at it—and yes—obsessed with it. I've been snowboarding forever. In fact, I can't remember a time when I didn't snowboard.

Truthfully, I only like doing things that I'm good at. My English teacher, Mrs. Cruickshank, thinks this is a problem. She only thinks so because I'm not very good at English, so I hate it. She is sure that I'm better than a C student.

This past year, we've been working on finding themes in the books we're reading. I haven't found any yet. I sometimes feel like throwing my book at the window. Instead, I pretend I am snowboarding and space out. Daydreaming is a lot better than a broken window, right? Mrs. Cruickshank doesn't seem to think so.

Ask my science teacher, Mr. Low, though, and he'll say that I'm doing fine in class. Better than fine, even. You see, I love science. I love learning how everything around us works. I'm the top student in his class! I got an A-plus last semester. Mr. Low said that I was going to be a great doctor someday.

I'm not sure if I want to be a doctor when I grow up. But I do know that I want to do something important, unlike my dad. My dad's real name is Martin Chadwick Morgan. To everyone in most of Wyoming, he's Mad Marty in the Morning. Dad hosts the Mad Marty Morning radio show on 104.5 FM. He describes his show as "a warm cup of wacky wake up on your way to work."

My dad's show is the number one morning radio show in Wyoming. Most kids at school think I'm lucky. They think having a semi-celebrity dad would make me proud. To be honest, I love my dad and I am proud of him. But a lot of times, he really embarrasses me.

Dads aren't supposed to invent new radio contests that involve bouncy balls. They aren't supposed to scuba dive in giant pools of chocolate pudding. And they aren't supposed to compete in hot dog eating contests.

Dads are supposed to be more like my mom—responsible and serious. My mom is vice president of Snow Leopard Gear. The company is the fourth-largest manufacturer of outdoor clothing in the world. She's not a local celebrity like dad, but she is very important to the company.

It's not totally perfect having such a responsible and serious mom either. There's a lot to do when you're vice president of a huge company. Mom works all the time. Plus, she goes on lots of business trips to places like China and Switzerland. Once she went to Iceland. She was gone for two months!

When she's not traveling, she might as well be gone anyway. She's in the office every day, even on weekends. Most nights I go to bed before she even comes home. My mom started working at Snow Leopard designing jackets and worked her way up. She's very determined and driven. I really admire her, but most of the time I just miss her.

So those are my parents. Although my life isn't perfect, I'm a pretty happy person. I *do* have two of the best friends a person could ever ask for. One is Sally Peterson. The other is Oscar the Wonder Poodle. Sally and I have been friends since we were in diapers. We do everything together, except snowboard. Sally's not really an outdoors type of person. Still, she comes to most of my races to cheer me on. That's how good a friend she is.

And then there's Oscar. Oscar is a standard poodle, but there's nothing standard about him. He doesn't have one of those poofy haircuts like most poodles have. Oscar is rugged and loves being outside. He loves going on walks and playing in the snow. Plus, when you talk to him, he stares right at you. Oscar's the best dog in the world. He understands everything I say to him.

CHAPTER THREE

THE PHONE CALL

The phone rang at 7:34 in the morning. I knew it wasn't for me. Sally is the only person who ever calls me. It couldn't have been her. She was asleep in the bed on the other side of the room. The loud ringing woke me, along with Sally and Oscar. We had been up late the night before, watching movies and talking. A phone call at 7:34 on a Sunday morning was not my idea of a good time.

My parents get lots of phone calls for work. From the pieces of the conversation I overheard, I knew this call was for Dad. "Yes hello . . . no it's fine . . . uh huh, uh huh . . . huh? You're joking!" My dad's voice got louder. "You're kidding! Leave Wyoming? Well, I never thought about it. They want us when? Next week! Uh, huh . . . uh huh . . . Well, that sounds great! Thank you so much. Los Angeles, here we come!"

I shot up from the bed, fully awake. I looked at Oscar, then Sally. I couldn't believe what I just heard. Did Sally hear it too?

"Did my dad just say Los Angeles here we come?"

"I don't think so," said Sally. She seemed half asleep still.

"I'm sure that's what he said. We're moving to Los Angeles next week." I started to panic. "I can't move to Los Angeles. There are too many people in Los Angeles. There's no snowboarding in Los Angeles. You are too far away from Los Angeles. I can not move to Los Angeles."

"Calm down, Cece. You're not moving anywhere." Sally sat up and stretched her arms. "Remember when you thought you got the black lung disease, but it was just dust making you sneeze? This is the same thing. You're not moving to Los Angeles," she laughed, as if it was no big deal.

This calmed me down. After all, Sally had a good point. I do tend to overreact. She was always able to get me to relax. "Maybe you're right. But I swear that's what I heard." I threw my covers off and got out of bed. "Before I officially start freaking, I'll check it out. It's probably nothing." I opened my door and whispered, "I'll be right back."

I stepped quietly into the hallway. As I approached my parent's door, I could hear them fighting. It was a noise that I had gotten used to. Lately, they fought whenever they were together. They tried to hide it from me, but that was pointless. I could hear them through the vent in my room. Besides, I could always tell when they had been arguing anyway. After a fight, my dad would be extra-special nice to me. Meanwhile, my mom would get really quiet. Sometimes she would even leave the house for a few hours. Same thing every time.

Carefully, I put my ear up to their door. I could hear everything: "What am I supposed to do? Just pack up and leave my job?" my mom asked.

"This is the opportunity of a lifetime."

"This is the opportunity of *your* lifetime."

"This is good for all of us."

"How is moving to the worst city in America good for all of us?"

"I don't think that's fair."

"What am I going to do in Los Angeles? I can't just ask the company to move over there. I've worked eleven years to get where I am. Am I just supposed to walk away from it?"

"Can't you even be the least bit happy for me? This is a dream come true."

"Have you thought about your daughter? Can you imagine how she's going to handle this? Los Angeles, Martin?"

This was not good. For the first time in my life, I was right, not over-reacting. I stood frozen outside my parent's bedroom. I simply couldn't move.

"I have to get out of here for a while," I heard my mom say. Suddenly the door swung open. My mom was surprised to see me. "Oh, Cece," she said.

I stood quiet for a second. "The phone woke me up."

"I guess you heard then?" My mom did not look at all happy. "You heard everything?"

I nodded.

My dad appeared behind her, looking serious. "Well, I guess we should all talk about this." He didn't make a joke. I knew right then, that this was for real.

A few minutes later, Mom and I drove Sally home. I don't think Sally really understood what was happening. She actually seemed excited about the whole situation. We both sat in the back seat. "Do you think you're going to live next door to a movie star? I wonder who it's gonna be."

"Not now, Sally."

"I just can't believe this. I can't wait to visit. I've been waiting my whole life to get out of this town. Now, you're really doing it, Cece! Los Angeles!" My mom shot Sally a scowling look. Sally was quiet for the rest of the ride.

When Mom and I got back, we sat at the kitchen table with Dad. I couldn't remember the last time we had all been together like this. At first, everyone just stared at something silently. Dad looked at Mom. She stared out the window. I focused on the kitchen table.

I hated that kitchen table. The tiles were all different shapes, sizes, and colors. It was really ugly.

"I'm sorry you heard all of that," my dad said, looking at me.

Mom nodded.

Dad kept talking. "I guess it's good that we all found out about this together. That way we can decide about this as a family."

I stared at the disgusting table.

"Now, your father will to try to convince us to move," my mother remarked.

"Let's try to be helpful here," my father countered.

"I just don't see how this is going to be a *conversation.* It's clear that you are going to move no matter what."

"That's not true."

I kept looking at the table. I really didn't want to be a part of this.

"Oh, really? You're going to call and say, 'My wife and daughter don't want to leave. Thanks for the offer, but I think I'm going to pass.' That's what could come out of this discussion?" Mom stared out the window and shook her head.

I was lost, staring at the tiles.

Mom stood up. "Cece, I'm sorry you're in the middle of this. I'm going for a walk." And with that, my mom left the house. She didn't exactly slam the door, but she closed it with force. It was just me and my dad and the kitchen table.

We sat in silence. "So, Chili, what do you think about all this?"

"Huh?" I couldn't think of anything to say. Too many things were going on in my head. Too much was happening.

"How would you feel about moving to Los Angeles?"

When he put it like that, I snapped: "Terrible. Miserable. Horrible. That's how I'd feel." I said this matter-of-factly. Then I jumped up from the table and ran into my room. I slammed the door as hard as I could behind me. Oscar jumped up from my bed, scared. I pet him to calm him down. Then I started crying.

At that moment, I knew I'd be moving to Los Angeles in a week. There was nothing I could say or do about it. Dad's mind was made up. All of my begging wouldn't going to change anything. We were going to move. My dad was going to take his dream job in Los Angeles.

For the rest of that night Dad did his best to be nice to me. He tried to tell me how I should keep an open mind. "There's a reason so many people live in Los Angeles, Cece. It's a great place." I refused to listen to him. He only wanted me to be excited so he wouldn't feel guilty about destroying my life.

CHAPTER FOUR

CECE AND SALLY

"You can stay with me," Sally said. "My parents love you. Or I could go instead of you."

Sally and I were sitting on the swings at Homestead Park. We spent a lot of time there. The park has two swings, a slide, and monkey bars. Because it's so small, nobody really goes there. Except Sally and me. We meet there when we need to talk about important stuff. There's also little patch of grass for Oscar to run around on. It's our perfect secret meeting place.

We sat in silence for a minute. Then I looked down at Oscar, who was lying down. "What do you think about all of this, boy?"

He tilted his head to let me know that he understood.

"He'll have fun in LA," Sally said.

I smiled, "Yeah, I bet he will. A beautiful poodle

like him will fit in better me." I kicked my feet in the patch of dirt that was worn away under the swing.

"Wait a minute, you can't go." This was the moment it finally hit Sally. I was *really* moving. Until now, she hadn't seriously thought about what moving meant. "You can't break up Cece and Sally. We were supposed to be together forever. You can't leave me alone." Sally looked down at her feet. "It's going to be awful without you here. This isn't fair."

"I know."

Sally was quiet. She kept staring at her feet, kicking at the dirt. She looked back up at me. Tears were streaming down her cheek. "This really stinks."

"Come on, Sally. LA's not that far away. We'll write. There's the phone, e-mail, and you can come visit me in the summer. We'll go to Disneyland, Universal Studios, Hollywood, Beverly Hills. And you never know what famous neighbor I might have." I couldn't stand to see Sally upset.

"What about snowboarding?" she asked.

That was the magic question. I paused for a while before I spoke. "Well," I finally said, "it will give me an excuse to come home all the time." We smiled at each other.

When Sally left the park she seemed to be feeling a little better. I went home and felt worse. Disneyland, Universal Studios, Beverly Hills—these things sounded great, but they weren't me. I was a snowboarder from Wyoming, not a Californian.

By the time I got to my front door, I was near tears. I couldn't imagine a life without the mountains. I couldn't imagine a life without snowboarding. That's when I decided to check something out. I mean, there had to be *some* snowboarding near Los Angeles. It wasn't like I was moving to the moon.

I went online. I soon found that the closest mountain—Big Bison—was three hours from Los Angeles. That was pretty far, but at least there was someplace I could go to snowboard. I decided to give them a call.

"Big Bison."

"Yeah, hi. How much snow do you have at your base right now?"

"Uh, I don't know," said the clueless guy on the other end.

"If you had to guess, what would you say?"

He paused for a long time. "Why would I have toguess?"

"Let's say that someone was calling you on the phone, right?'

"Yeah," he answered.

This might have been the stupidest person I had ever spoken to. "Okay. Well, pretend that this person was wondering how much snow there was on your mountain. What would you tell her?"

"I'd probably put Steve on the phone," he said.

"Okay, can I speak to Steve?" I asked.

"Steve's not working today."

"Well, thanks, bye." I quickly hung up the phone. It was looking like snowboarding was out of the picture for good. In less than a week I'd be losing my two favorite things: snowboarding and Sally. Thanks a lot, Dad.

I didn't see how things could get worse, but somehow they did. Right after I hung up, my parents called me downstairs for another meeting. I asked them this time if we could sit in the living room. I couldn't handle staring at the kitchen table again.

My dad began. "Cece, your mother and I have been doing some talking. This show is a dream come true for me. I can't pass up the opportunity. On the other hand, your mother's job right now is her dream. She's worked very hard to get to where she is."

"That's right," my mom cut in.

"So we've decided that you and I are going to go out to Los Angeles first. We'll check things out. It'll be fun. I promise. School will just be starting its spring term, so it will be. . . "

"Mom's not coming?" I asked, looking at my dad. "You're not coming with us?" I stared over at my mom. She stared back at me with tears in her eyes.

Dad continued, "She's going to continue her job here, Cece."

"Well, I want to stay too." I said.

Mom chimed in, "It's not that simple, Cece. With your dad gone, there would be nobody to look after you. My work schedule is just too crazy."

"I can look after myself."

Dad continued, "This is the only way it's going to work, Chili. Mom will start looking for work in Los Angeles. When she finds something as good as what she has here, she'll join us."

She's never going to move to Los Angeles, I thought. I'm never going to see my mother again.

"I know it will be hard for a while, Cece," Mom said. "But this is the best we can do right now."

I didn't see how splitting up the family would be best. I couldn't think too hard about it, or I would start crying again. Just me and Dad. Well, I guess that's kind of the way it's been lately anyway.

"Cece, what do you think?" Dad asked.

I looked at my parents, sitting across the room from each other. My vision was blurred by tears. "Do you really want to know what I think?"

"Yes," they spoke at the same time.

"Okay," I said, as I stared at my father. "You're selfish, Dad. You also don't *really* care what I think. You make your decisions based on what *you* think." I looked at my mother, "I guess this is perfect for you, Mom. Now you can spend all your time at work. You never have to see me and Dad." Those comments were the meanest things I had ever said. Speaking the hurtful words made me start crying. So I left the room, heading upstairs to grab Oscar for a walk.

When I came back downstairs, my parents were still in the living room. They were silent.

CHAPTER FIVE

THE REARVIEW MIRROR

The next two weeks flew by like a tornado—fast and out of control.

I'd never had to pack before, so this was a new experience. I barely knew what to do. I organized everything with one giant cardboard box for each category of my stuff. I labeled one "tops," which included anything I wore on the top half of my body. Of course, I had a box labeled "bottoms" as well. This included everything I wore on the bottom half of my body. I had a separate box labeled "feet." I had too many shoes to fit in the "bottoms" box. I also had one entire box that was filled with snowboard stuff. I labeled that box "just in case."

My entire life, twelve years, fit in ten boxes. I guess that's because I don't keep very much stuff. I've always kept my Three Special Things with me, though. It seems silly, but they are really important to me.

The first of my Three Special Things is a pair of Mom's glasses. Before Mom got laser eye surgery, she could barely see. Sometimes I put on her glasses and everything gets all fuzzy.

The second special thing is an orange coated in plastic. I won it at the Wyoming State Fair when I was six. This booth at the fair had a penny jar. Whoever guessed closest to how many pennies were in the jar won the pennies. The winner also took home a plastic-coated orange. There were 643 pennies in the jar. I guessed 637. The guy behind the booth said the orange inside the plastic really is an actual orange. It's a strange prize, but I've always kept it with me. It's the first thing I ever won.

My third special thing is a framed picture of my parents at their wedding. They're dancing. My dad is dipping my mom. Mom is wearing a big beautiful white wedding dress. Dad is wearing a blue tuxedo that he swears was cool at the time. They're both smiling and look so happy in the picture.

I'm not sure why I keep these things, I just do. I keep them in my nightstand drawer. No one but Oscar knows them. It's just too embarrassing to tell anyone else how important they are to me.

When I finally finished boxing everything up, I walked around my empty room. There were marks in the carpet from where my furniture had stood. I sat down and ran my fingers along the carpet lines. I sat there on the floor for about an hour, I guess. I wasn't thinking about anything in particular. I felt numb.

I probably could have sat there forever. A nudge in my back snapped me out of it. Oscar was behind me, with one of my snowboarding gloves in his mouth. "Hey, boy," I said, scratching his ears. "Where'd you get that?" I took the glove from his mouth. "What a great idea."

Oscar barked once in response. I told you my dog is a genius, right?

The next thing I knew I was tearing apart the box labeled "just in case." I had to hit the slopes one last time before I left. *Just in case* I never came back.

Fifteen minutes later, I was standing at the top of the Big Chill. I strapped on my binding like I'd done a million times before. This time it felt weird, though.

It was a perfect day to snowboard. The sun was shining and there was about a foot of new powder. Normally, I would be in heaven on a day like this. Not today, though. I couldn't shake this feeling I had. A feeling that I was losing something. I tried to ignore it as I began my run down the mountain.

I started to snap out of it as soon as I began to pick up speed. It was hard not to feel great when I was on the mountain. I was in total control up here. My board did exactly what I wanted it to do. I sliced through the snow like I was riding a giant razor.

The tracks I left behind were in the shapes of perfect Cs, like my name. CC was here. CC was here. CC was here.

The next day was my last day of school in Rockville. It was actually pretty boring. I think Mrs. Cruickshank was glad to see me go. I was a big pain to her. I will miss Mr. Low, though. When science class ended, he shook my hand. "Looks like Hollywood's getting a good doctor," he said.

The weirdest thing about leaving school that day was that it *didn't* feel weird. It actually felt kind of good. I hadn't made very many close friends here. Besides Sally, most of the friends I'd made were people I'd met snowboarding. I never quite fit in at school. In a way, I was glad to be leaving it behind. It was as if I'd gotten a free pass to start all over somewhere else. Maybe there was at least one good thing about moving. Maybe going to school in Los Angeles would be better for me.

That feeling lasted twenty-one hours. That's when it was finally time to say goodbye to Sally for real. I was not looking forward to this. I got by most of the time by pretending it wasn't going to happen.

Mom, Dad, and I had loaded up the car. We were all packed up when Sally walked up our driveway. "Cece," she said, "were you going to leave without saying goodbye?" She looked upset.

I guess I really *was* going to leave without saying good-bye. "No," I lied.

Sally looked at me blankly.

I smiled so I wouldn't cry. "So, where's *your* stuff?" I asked.

"Come on, Cece. That isn't funny."

That's what did it. Not thinking about leaving Sally couldn't change what was going to happen. I was moving. Sally wasn't. All the sadness I was holding back came out all at once. I started sobbing right there in my driveway.

This set off Sally and she lost it too. We were falling apart in my front yard. I was doing those big heaving sobs. Sally's were shorter, but much louder.

"Sally . . . I'm . . . going . . . to . . . miss . . . you . . . so . . . much." I managed to get out.

"It's not fair!" she sobbed back.

We hugged each other and stayed that way for a while. Hugging and crying. Crying and hugging. Eventually, we calmed down and broke apart. I didn't know what to say. Sally reached into her pocket and pulled out a small round package. It was wrapped in shiny gold paper and tied with a red bow.

"What is it?" I asked, wiping the tears off my cheek.

Sally shrugged. "Open it later, okay?"

My dad opened the front door. "Well, Cece, it's time to hit the road." He looked at Sally. "Do you want a ride home, Sally?"

"No thanks, Mr. Morgan. I'm going to head

the park for a while."

A moment later, my mom came out the front door. She gave me a hug. "I'll see you soon. Things are going to be okay." I was so upset that I couldn't say anything back to her.

Sally was still standing next to our car. I was about to lose it again, so I got in and shut the door.

"Girls," my dad said, "I know this is difficult now, but Los Angeles isn't far away. And, Sally, I spoke to your parents. They've agreed to let you visit us there. We'll have a blast." I looked at Sally and smiled. "You guys have too good a friendship to let distance get in the way," Dad said. "It'll work out." When he wanted to, Dad could really make me feel better.

He opened the door for Oscar and rolled up the window. We pulled out of the driveway and gave a final wave. I couldn't turn back. Instead, I stared at the rearview mirror as we drove away. Dad honked a few times. My mother, my house, and my best friend got smaller and smaller. Soon, they all faded out of sight.

That's when I reached into my pocket. I pulled out Sally's present. I unwrapped it carefully. At first, I didn't know what the little round disc was. The circle was about the size of a coaster that you put drinks on, and was wrapped in plastic. I flipped it over. The sticker on the back read: Mr. Fatty Waves Surf Wax. I smiled. It was wax for a surfboard. There was a tiny card taped to the label. I opened it. "If you can't ride the mountains, you might as well ride the waves."

"What's that?" asked my dad.

"Nothing," I said. I leaned back in the seat.

As the road blurred by us, I closed my eyes and smiled. Everyone should have a friend like Sally.

CHAPTER SIX

ENTERING LOS ANGELES

It took two days to get to California. Along the way we passed through Wyoming, Utah, and Nevada. I slept through a lot of the ride. When I *was* up, Oscar and I usually just looked out the window. Everything around us was flat. It seemed to go on forever, in every direction.

Everything changed when we got close to Los Angeles. Things started to get more and more developed. We passed one crowded town after another. The freeway kept getting wider, too. It seemed like every time we drove another ten miles, another lane appeared. The wider the road got, the more cars there were on it. I had never seen so many cars. I felt trapped. I could tell Dad was getting nervous too. Years of driving in snow hadn't prepared him for moving through ten lanes of traffic.

The car climbed a pretty steep hill. When we finally reached the top, we passed a sign that read: Entering Los Angeles, population three million, six-hundred and ninety-four thousand, eight hundred and twenty. Dad read it out loud, but he added three more to the total: three million, six-hundred and ninety-four thousand, eight hundred and twenty three. Now that he and Oscar and I had arrived. I laughed out loud.

We drove about forty-five more minutes. Everywhere you looked, there were people and more people. The roads were everywhere too. Back home, there were two main roads going through downtown. Here, there were too many stoplights to count. The concrete went on forever.

We got off the freeway and stopped at an intersection that connected eight different roads. It was confusing. I was trying to help my dad, but I couldn't understand the map.

I stared out the window as we waited for the light to change. Next to a fancy sports car stood a bearded homeless man. He was begging for spare change. A group of people on motor scooters passed us. Billboards in different languages were everywhere. Oscar was running around in circles in the back seat. His nose was going crazy with all the strange new smells.

I couldn't get over how fast the neighborhoods changed. We'd pass one block and all the apartments would be run down. Two blocks later, there'd be fancy cars parked in front of nice buildings.

We eventually drove into a nice neighborhood that stayed nice. The street was lined with palm trees. This was what LA looked like in all the movies I had seen. I had to admit, it was beautiful.

My dad double-checked an address he had written down. He then made a left turn and pulled up to a gate. He rolled down the window. "Here we are, Chili," he said. He punched some numbers into a little metal box. The gate swung open and we drove into a large round driveway. The only word I could use to describe our new house was "Whoa!"

I guess having a big time radio show pays off.

When we opened the front door, we were impressed right away. The house was beautiful. Though we were excited, Dad and I were both ready to sleep. We decided to head to our bedrooms and check out the rest of the house in the morning. My bedroom was awesome! It had high ceilings and in the left corner there was a skylight.

When I woke up that next morning, the sun was shining on my bed. A breeze was blowing and some birds were chirping. Even through the glass, I could feel the strength of the Los Angeles sun. Oscar loved it.

"You like the skylight?" I asked.

He shook his tail, which means yes.

Besides the skylight, there are three windows in my room. One looks out into the backyard—which is beautiful. The first thing I noticed when I checked it out was the pool. I could not believe that we had our own pool!

While looking out the window, I saw my Dad in the yard. He noticed me watching him and waved. Then he put down his coffee mug and ran into the pool. He made a huge splash. The holler he let out as he hit the water probably woke our neighbors. I quickly threw on my suit and ran outside to join him. By the time I got out there, Oscar was swimming too. I had no idea he liked the water.

I glanced around the yard as I floated toward Dad. We had a lot of lemon trees, which smelled fantastic. Plus, there were rows of tropical looking flowers in front of the lemon tress. Hanging from one of the lemon trees was a hummingbird feeder. So far, I had seen four hummingbirds. Hummingbirds are amazing. Their wings flap so fast that you can't even see them. When I spoke to Sally later, the first thing I told her about was the hummingbirds.

That weekend in our new house was great. Dad, Oscar, and I had a really good time. I even forgot for a little while that I was mad. Oscar loved the backyard, but the pool was his favorite. I loved being in the water too.

I put off thinking about my new school until Sunday. I used my old trick, convincing myself that I wouldn't have to go for a while. Deep down, I knew I was going to have to face the reality eventually. And I knew it wasn't going to be easy. Being the new kid is hard for anyone. But I knew this task would be extra hard on me. I'd barely made any friends at my old school, and I'd lived in Rockville my whole life.

Before I knew it, Sunday night arrived. School was less than twelve hours away. I stood in my room, looking into the empty backyard. It was warm, but a cool breeze flowed through my hair from my open window. It felt good. I was doing my best to try and be calm about tomorrow. Maybe Los Angeles wasn't going to be that bad.

CHAPTER SEVEN

NEW SCHOOL DISASTER

My hopes of things being better were soon flushed down the toilet. I have to say, some people in LA are not like my beautiful backyard. They are not calm and peaceful. They are not nice and pretty. They are mean and ugly.

Anyway, here's what happened. I tried to be excited about the first day of school. It was really hard, though. Even getting dressed was stressful. I laid out as many different outfit possibilities with the clothes I had. I looked at the combinations on the floor. I suddenly realized that my Wyoming clothes might not fit in very well in LA. There was nothing wrong with them—they just weren't LA. What I mean is, there wasn't anything special or outrageous about them. Oscar watched as I walked back and forth, looking at my different outfits.

"What do you think, boy?" I asked, holding up khaki pants and a striped pink and yellow shirt. This was one of my coolest shirts back home. He shook his head in disapproval. In matters of fashion, always listen to a poodle.

"Yeah, I know. I don't know what to do, though."

I obsessed about it until the very last minute. In the end, I decided my simplest outfit would probably be best. I would go with a white v-neck t-shirt and my best jeans. If I couldn't fit in, I should be as invisible as possible.

My first day started off well enough. No one paid much attention to me. But I definitely paid attention to them. Students at David Hasselhoff Middle School looked different from the kids from Wyoming. I couldn't believe I was the same age as they were. Most girls wore tight shirts that showed their stomachs and lots of makeup too. They looked like they could have been in college. The boys' hair was so spiky it looked like weapons.

My first class of the day was English, my least favorite subject. My teacher, though, Mrs. Blossom, was really cool. She was younger than any teacher I've ever had. Her hair was dark brown with cool blonde streaks running though it. She smiled at me when I walked in. "You must be Cecelia. Welcome to David Hasselhoff and welcome to English."

"Thank you," I said. "You can call me Cece."

"I'm glad you're here a little early, Cece. I'd like to introduce you to the class. But I wanted to make sure you were cool with the introduction. No sense embarrassing you on the first day, right?" She smiled at me again. I never had a teacher who talked like Mrs. Blossom. She talked liked a kid. I felt comfortable with her right away. "So, you just moved here from Wisconsin, right?"

"Wyoming," I corrected her.

"Great. What do you think of LA so far?"

"It's a lot different from home," I said.

"It took me a few years to get used to it here. But if you give it a chance, it'll grow on you."

"I hope so."

The bell rang. I was so focused on talking to Mrs. Blossom that I didn't realize the class had filled up. "I guess we should get started," said Mrs. Blossom, giving me a little wink. She showed me my seat. To my right was a skinny African American guy named Hershel. He couldn't stop smiling. I knew his name was Hershel because it was stitched into his collared shirt. He made eye contact with me the moment he walked in. I could tell that he had the most friend potential of anyone I had seen.

Mrs. Blossom's class began. "All right people, we've got lots to do today. I'd like to introduce you to a new student—this is Cece Morgan."

The whole class shouted, "Welcome, Cece!"

I turned a little red, but for a good type of embarrassment.

"Cece just moved here from Wyoming," said Mrs. Blossom. "So you can imagine how big of a change Los Angeles is for her. I know we'll all give an extra-special effort to make her feel welcome."

Hershel turned to me with another huge smile. "I think I speak for the entire class when I bid you farewell to Wyoming, the Cowboy State. I'd like offer you the sunniest of welcomes to California, the Golden State." I smiled from ear to ear. Hershel was strange, but he was super nice.

For the rest of the class, Mrs. Blossom talked about adverbs. Normally, I would be bored, but Mrs. Blossom was a great teacher. A single girl sitting in the back, though, seemed completely bored. She was picking at her fingernails. I noticed that each nail was painted a different shade of pink. I didn't even know that there were ten shades of pink. She was dressed in the same tiny-shirt outfit that seemed to be the uniform here.

She noticed me looking at her and looked up from her nails to glare at me. Her stare made me want to crawl inside my backpack and never come out. I quickly turned away from her. I could tell this was the kind of person you didn't want to mess with. Without meaning to, I had just gotten on her bad side.

The class ended. I stood in the hall trying to find room 204. Just then, I felt a hard tap on my shoulder. When I turned around Ms. Perfect Pretty Pink Nails was standing next to me. "Why were you staring at me in class?" she asked rudely.

"Excuse me?"

"I asked you why you were staring at me. Are you hard of hearing or just stupid?"

"No, um, I'm not," I said, totally shocked by this comment.

"Not what? Hard of hearing, or stupid?"

By this time, a small crowd had gathered around Ms. Perfect Pretty Pink Nails. This was not what I needed on my first day. I started to get really nervous. Why was this girl picking on me? I didn't do anything to her. "Neither," I managed to get out.

"So then, why were you staring at me?"

I didn't know what she wanted from me. "I'm not sure what you want from me." I confessed.

"Things are different here, Ms. Wyoming. And we have rules—like no staring!"

"Oh, okay," I said. I stood there helplessly. I didn't know what to do or where to go. "I'll keep that in mind." I said, as I tried to walk away.

She stood in front of me. There was no escaping her. "So," she continued, "what are we going to do about our problem?"

"I don't really think we have a problem," I said, trying to get away. "What we have is a misunderstanding."

She got right up in my face. "No, we definitely have a problem, Wyoming freak! You show up in horrible clothes and act like you can do whatever you want. You really are stupid!"

It was then that I did the worst possible thing. I started crying—right in front of everyone. And of course she did what all mean girls do in those situations—she laughed. A crowd of girls who looked, and dressed, exactly like her joined in. I felt trapped. I was certain that I was going to be standing there forever, crying.

"Portia, what's going on here?" I heard an adult voice through the crowd.

Ms. Perfect Pretty Pink Nails' smile turned to a look of panic. Mrs. Blossom made her way through all of the kids.

"Nothing, Mrs. Blossom." said Portia, or whatever her name was.

"This looks like more than nothing," said Mrs. Blossom. She watched me wipe the tears on my check away with my palm. Her face became angry.

"It's okay, Mrs. Blossom," I spoke up. "I'm just homesick. It's a lot different here in Los Angeles. Portia didn't do anything."

Portia looked at me like I was crazy. Mrs. Blossom didn't believe me, but she knew what I was trying to do. If I got Portia into trouble now, she would make my life in Los Angeles miserable. I was just trying to get her off my back.

"Okay, but if you have any problems, Cece, you can talk to me." Mrs. Blossom said.

"Thank you," I said forcing a smile.

By this time, most people had cleared away. I was able to walk to my next class. But I didn't. Instead, I marched straight into the girls' bathroom. I opened up the first stall, locking it behind me. To my relief, the bathroom was empty. Sitting there alone, I got the rest of my crying out.

CHAPTER EIGHT

THE MAGICIAN

My crying was interrupted a moment later. "Cece?" I heard someone say my name, softly. How did anyone here know my name? And how did anyone know I was in the bathroom? And why did it sound like a boy's voice?

"Cece?" I heard the voice again.

The voice definitely didn't belong to Portia, so I answered. "Yeah."

"It's me, Hershel, from English class. Are you okay?"

"What are you doing in here?" I asked, as I opened the door. "This is the girls' room."

"You're upset. I thought I'd try to make you feel better." Hershel answered me as if standing in the girls' bathroom was normal.

"Why do you care?" I asked, defensively.

"Because," he whispered, "a year ago, when I moved here, I used to get picked on." He paused, then raised his voice a bit. "They were picking on Hershel, last year! So, I know how you're feeling—not excellent." Then, he reached into his pocket and pulled out a deck of cards. He fanned them out in front of me. "Pick a card," he said.

"Excuse me?" I asked.

"Pick a card," he said again. "But don't show me."

I did as Hershel said. He grinned as I pulled an eight of diamonds from the deck.

"Got your card?"

I nodded.

"Excellent, now put it back in the deck, anywhere. Careful, don't show me what it is."

I put the card back in the deck.

Hershel shuffled the cards. "I'm shuffling the cards here. Now if I could pick your card from this single shuffle, it would be impressive. But for you, I'm going for amazing." Hershel handed me the deck of cards. "I'm going to turn around and I'd like you to shuffle the cards."

He turned around. I shuffled the deck a few times.

"Are you finished?" Hershel asked.

"All done," I said.

Hershel turned back around and I handed him the shuffled cards.

"If I could pick out your card now, it would be amazing, right?"

"Right," I smiled.

"But if I was able to pick your card after doing *this*. . . " Hershel dropped the cards onto the bathroom floor. He spread the cards around with his hands. "It would arguably be the most excellent trick in the galaxy, right?"

It would certainly be the most disgusting trick in the galaxy, I thought. "Right."

Hershel gathered up the deck from the bathroom floor. I really hoped he wasn't going to make me touch the cards again. He shuffled through the deck for what seemed like five minutes. He finally stopped. "Prepare to be dazzled," he said as he flashed a three of clubs in my face.

"That's not my card," I said.

"That's impossible," replied Hershel.

"I'm sorry, but that's not my card." I was laughing now.

"Of course that's not your card." He smiled.

Once again, Hershel fumbled through the cards. He pulled another card from the deck—a ten of hearts. "Amazing, right?"

"That's not my card either," I said again.

"Hmmm," said Hershel. "This must be a rare case where I can't read my participant's mind. Being in the girls' bathroom must be disrupting me somehow."

"Must be," I said.

"Anyway," said Hershel, putting the deck of cards back in his pocket. "Don't let Portia get to you. There are plenty of nice people here."

"Thanks, Hershel," I said. I wanted to give him a hug but decided not to.

"It's my pleasure." He bowed. "Hershel the famous magician is late for class." And with that, he left the bathroom.

A few minutes later, I left too. Thanks to Hershel, I was feeling much better now. But that feeling lasted only about three seconds. That's how long it was before Portia stood in front of me again in the hallway. "Hey, freak, where do you think you're going?"

"Art," I said.

"Well, before you go, I don't want you getting the wrong idea."

"What do you mean?"

"Just because you got Blossom off my back doesn't mean that I like you."

Again, I found myself not knowing what to say.

"We had enough freaks here before you showed up." She pushed her finger into my chest, "I'm going to make sure that you never get comfortable, freak."

She walked away, laughing with her friends. It was amazing how a complete stranger could make me feel so bad about myself. The next thing I knew I was back in the bathroom crying. I wished that Hershel knew a magic trick that would make Portia disappear.

CHAPTER NINE

THE BIG BLUE OCEAN

My dad was waiting for me when school finally got out. The bell rang at three thirty. I felt like I was being released from prison. He sat in the driver's seat with a giant grin on his face. After we left the parking lot, he turned to me and asked, "How was it?"

Seeing him sitting there with that big, stupid grin made me lose it. "It was the worst day of my entire life!" I screamed at him.

"What happened?" he asked, slowing the car to a stop.

"Why would you care?" I snapped at him.

"Come on, Chili, I want to know what happened."

"No you don't. You just want me to be quiet so that you don't have to feel guilty. I told you I was going to hate it here, but I was wrong. They hate me!

We're not supposed to be here, Dad." I was yelling and crying at the same time. I couldn't hold back. "I want to go home!"

"I'm sorry you had such a terrible day, Chili," said my dad. "Will you please tell me about it?"

"You're not sorry enough to move back, are you?"

"Honey, you have to give it more than one day."

"Why? I know it's not going to get better. I'm never going to fit in here. I don't want to fit in here!"

We drove in silence for a few minutes. I closed my eyes, wishing that things were different. Dad broke the silence. "Let's go see the ocean. Maybe that will make you feel a little better."

Twenty minutes later, we were staring at sign that read: Dolly Parton State Park. Everything in Los Angeles seemed to be named after a celebrity.

When we got out of the car I noticed that the air was different. It smelled cleaner than the air outside of David Hasselhoff Middle School. It also had a taste. It was salty. Right away, I could feel something inside of me change. The frustration, sadness, and anger were gone. I was excited to be by the ocean.

I stood on my tip-toes to catch a glimpse. I couldn't see it yet because of a big pile of sand in front of the parking lot. I kicked off my shoes and started running toward the giant sand dune. Dad quickly took off his fancy shoes and ran up the hill behind me.

The sand made me run slowly. My feet sunk a few inches with every step I took. I felt a little like I was walking in deep snow. I liked the familiar—yet different—feeling. As I reached the sand pile, I caught a glimpse of a big blue something. It was the ocean. I had never actually seen the ocean up close. It was amazing!

"Well Chili, there it is," Dad said.

"Wow! Those waves are awesome." We walked a little farther down the sand mound towards the water. I was mesmerized. The blue went on forever. There was no other side to the ocean. It was one big, beautiful thing, and it was alive. I felt alive just watching it. A wave would crash against the shore then return to the sea. Then another wave would come in. And another. And another. It never ended.

I felt the same rush as when I stood above an untracked run of fresh powder. I didn't feel sad. I wasn't even mad at my dad. I felt calm. I was just watching the ocean. I was totally happy.

I looked out at the endless blue. Staring at the ocean made my mind wander. I started to think about Oscar. I was sure that he would like the ocean. I pictured him swimming and smiled. In the middle of that random thought, something in the water caught my attention. I squinted at a group of people about a hundred yards out. I walked closer to the water. Dad followed right behind me.

When I figured out that they were surfing, my

heart started to really race. “Wow,” I said again, loudly, into the air. I watched powerful waves coming in with skilled surfers standing on them. It was so cool—they were riding the waves. They were riding the ocean. It reminded me of snowboarding, and I felt another jolt of excitement. This was the best I had felt since we got here.

“I’ve got to try that,” I whispered.

One surfer in particular caught my attention—a woman in a black and orange wetsuit. She was so graceful, catching one wave after another. She stayed on the waves much longer than everyone else. She carved big Cs with her board—CC, CC, CC. She was spelling out my name like I did when I was snowboarding. I wanted to be like this woman. I wanted to be like this woman who was waving at me. Why was this woman waving at me?

“Do you know that lady?” asked my dad.

“I don’t think so.”

She paddled to shore and walked up to us. As she got closer, I recognized her. It was Mrs. Blossom. Oh my gosh! She looked much different in a wetsuit than she did in class. “Hey, Cece,” she said, wringing water out of her hair.

“Hi, Mrs. Blossom,” I said. “Dad, this is my English teacher, Mrs. Blossom.”

My dad looked a little surprised. In Wyoming, he’d never seen any of my teachers in wetsuits. “Hello. I’m Marty Morgan,” he held out his hand. They shook.

"It's a pleasure to meet you."

"You look really great out there, Mrs. Blossom," I said.

"Thanks," she said. "The waves are pretty great today."

"Do you surf a lot?" I asked.

"As often as I can." She cleared her throat, "You know, we have a surf club at school. I encourage all my students to surf. There's nothing else like it on the planet."

"It looks like a lot of fun." I said.

Mrs. Blossom smiled. "We meet every Wednesday and Thursday afternoon, and Saturday morning. Beginners are welcome."

"That sounds great," Dad said.

I was actually getting excited about this surfing idea. "Yeah," I added.

"We've got extra wetsuits and a board you can borrow while you're learning.

Just bring a bathing suit with you to school. It will be great." Mrs. Blossom looked back out at the ocean. "Well, I'm heading back in. See you tomorrow, Cece. Nice meeting you," she said to my dad.

"Nice meeting you," Dad waved.

We watched her run back out into the ocean. Before we knew it, she was surfing again. Seeing Mrs. Blossom surf made me forget about how mad I was at Dad. I even forget about Portia, at least for a few minutes, anyway.

CHAPTER TEN

SURF'S UP

The next Wednesday finally arrived. It was going to be my first day participating in Surf Club. I was really eager to get on a surf board. When I had closed my eyes the night before, I imagined myself surfing. I was carving big, beautiful turns, like I did when I was on the mountain.

Before school, I crammed my green bathing suit into my book bag. I was actually excited about going to school.

Despite my enthusiasm, school was horrible, as usual. Portia and her crew were determined to make me miserable. Today, Mrs. Blossom handed back our English papers. Portia noticed that I got an A. As I walked out of class, she remarked, "Maybe you should spend less time studying and more time thinking about how you look. You are so gross."

"Yeah," one of her wannabes chimed in.

I guess I kind of built up a tolerance to Portia, because her comments weren't making me cry anymore. "Excuse me," I said as I walked though a group of her friends. In fact, for the first time, I had gone through an entire LA day without crying. I know that sounds awful, but at least I was making progress.

When the bell rang, I hurried to the parking lot. A bunch of kids were standing around in shorts and t-shirts. I didn't recognize most of them but I immediately spotted Hershel.

"Hi, Hershel," I said.

Hershel stuck out his hand and I shook it. "Cece, so glad you could make it." he smiled.

"I didn't know you surfed," I said.

"Oh yes," said Hershel. "I fence as well, and head up the math team. I'm starting a moon appreciation club next semester—the Lunar Club. You just have to love the moon. It's big, round, and it lights up the night sky. It's excellent."

"Cool," was the only reply I could come up with.

I stood with Hershel as all the other surfers talked in their own groups. Then Mrs. Blossom pulled up in a big white van. She stopped, jumped out, and opened the passenger door for us. "Next stop, tasty waves!" she said with a gigantic smile.

We all piled in the van. I was excited. It was the same excitement I used to feel on car rides to the mountain. The van moved a few feet and then stopped suddenly. The side door opened again. My heart sank as Portia and two of her clones climbed in. At least they aren't sitting near me, I thought.

As soon as the van started rolling, Hershel started talking. Wow, could he talk. At first, I did my best to listen. "Cece, the future in the pet industry lies in robotic monkeys. Think about it. It's a robot. It's a monkey. It's excellent. I'm confident this idea will break soon." He paused, but I didn't know what to say. "I call them chimpanpleases."

After getting through his chimpanplease idea, I started to pay only half-attention. I just couldn't keep up with his mouth. Luckily, he didn't seem to notice. He kept right on talking. The other half of my attention wandered around the van.

I noticed two boys sitting near Portia who were talking. Something made me keep looking—particularly at the boy on the left. As he spoke, he moved his hands up and down like he was imitating waves. Even from halfway across the van, I caught glimpses of his eyes. They were deep blue, like the waves I imagined he was talking about.

He turned around and his eyes met mine. I instantly felt two things: embarrassment, and a jolt of excitement. He looked at me! He noticed me. This was good. But, he noticed me because I was staring at him like a weirdo. This was bad. Our eyes met for a second time. He smiled. That little jolt of excitement turned into a lightening bolt. I could feel my face turning a shade of a tomato red. I quickly looked away and rejoined Hershel's talking marathon. "Just imagine the possibilities of a popsicle that stays cold but won't melt. It will change that way we think about frozen items on sticks."

"That sounds like a good idea, Hershel," I said.

"Thanks. I think so too."

Hershel stopped talking. "Are you okay, Cece? Your face is all red."

"Oh yeah, I'm fine. I just get a little flushed sometimes." I lied.

Hershel went right back to talking after that.

We eventually arrived at Dolly Parton State Park. I did my best to keep my distance from the boy with the blue eyes. And I stayed away from Portia. It wasn't that difficult with Hershel by my side. He was the perfect barrier. "We surf here because this water produces consistently excellent waves. Plus, there's a sandy bottom, which is what you want when you wipe out." We followed Mrs. Blossom from the parking lot onto the sand.

From snowboarding, I knew what it was like having to stay on a board at the right time. I was going to be fine. Hershel kept on talking as we walked. We climbed the little sand hill, and the big beautiful ocean came into view.

We approached a little pink hut in the middle of the beach. Mrs. Blossom looked up at the hut. "Hi

Pam," she said.

A tanned face with sunglasses leaned down. "Hey, Sonya." I guess Mrs. Blossom's first name was Sonya.

I had never seen a real-life lifeguard before. The lifeguards back home were always nerdy high school kids. Pam was completely different. She walked down the ramp to meet Mrs. Blossom. I stared at her as she approached us. Her arms and legs looked like they'd been carved from stone. I was impressed.

Pam opened a door under the lifeguard shack. Inside was a bunch of surfboards and wetsuits. "Suit up!" she said. Everyone made a mad rush, grabbing boards and wetsuits. I didn't know what to do, so I just stood there.

"Cece," said Mrs. Blossom, "we have a beginner's board I start all my new surfers on." She disappeared and came out with a gigantic board. "I know this looks clunky. Believe me, though, it's the best way to learn."

I studied the board for a second. It was this enormous faded green foam board. I looked over at the other kids suiting up. My board was at least twice as big as theirs. I thought about telling Mrs. Blossom about how good of a snowboarder I was. I was definitely good enough to start on a normal board. Then I decided to *wow* everyone on this easy board instead.

Soon, each of my classmates was suited up and had a board. Hershel was wearing this neon blue wetsuit that was probably two sizes too big. The large wetsuit made him look like he had gigantic muscles. He was a bright blue bodybuilding surfer. It was so funny. Hershel knew it too. He was doing all these fake weightlifting poses and everyone was laughing. You just had to love Hershel.

"Surf's up!" said Mrs. Blossom. "Everyone make sure that you can see Pam a at all times. If you can't see her, she can't see you. Now, what do you say we go ride the ocean?"

Everyone ran excitedly to the shore. I felt a jab on my shoulder. I turned around and there was Portia. "Stay out of my way, loser," she hissed.

Mrs. Blossom called after me before I could say anything back to Portia. "Cece, let's have a quick lesson."

I stopped. The rest of the class was already in the ocean. They started paddling on their surfboards. I really wanted to be out there. "Do you really think I need a lesson? I've done a ton of snowboarding in my life. And, I watched you surf before. I think I'll get the hang of it."

Mrs. Blossom laughed. "Trust me, Cece, we should have a quick lesson. Surfing is different from anything you've ever done. I'm sure you'll be great, we just need to go over a few things."

"Okay," I sighed.

"Put your board on the sand," said Mrs. Blossom.

I put the huge green board on the sand.

"Do you have any questions before we begin?"

"No," I said. I didn't want to tell Mrs. Blossom this was my first time in the ocean. I had always been a great swimmer.

"I'll start by telling you that catching a wave is one of the hardest things. It takes a lot of practice, and it takes learning the ocean. You see, waves come in sets. Some in the set are better than others. Some sets are better than others. Learning which wave to try to catch takes time to learn. It takes a lot of practice and patience. So don't be discouraged if you don't get it right away."

I understood what she was saying. I just didn't think it applied to me. *I* was an athlete.

Mrs. Blossom had me lie down on the board and then jump up to my feet. She had me do this over and over again. Once I was standing on the board, I was amazed at how wide it was. It was at least three times wider than my snowboard. "You don't have much time to get up on your board." she said. She had me jump up a few more times. "So you have to be ready to jump up. Okay?"

I nodded.

"Hey Pam," she shouted. "Will you keep one of your eyes on Cece?"

"No problem," said Pam.

Mrs. Blossom turned back to me. "Stay right there in front of Pam." Mrs. Blossom pointed to the area of water in front of the lifeguard shack. “Have fun!”

“Okay,” I said. “Thanks.”

I grabbed the big green board and headed to the ocean.

CHAPTER ELEVEN

COLLISION COURSE

I walked up to the shoreline. It was hard to move the board. It felt like I was carrying twenty snowboards. A wave came in and got me wet up to my shins. I took a deep breath. The water was freezing.

I got on top of the huge green board and paddled my arms like Mrs. Blossom had taught me on the beach. Okay, so this is the ocean, I thought to myself. It's no big deal. It's just a big salty lake. Suddenly, a bunch of white foamy water came rushing towards me. I tried as hard as I could to paddle through it. But the white water crashed into my face and knocked me off the board. I was shocked by how powerful the water was. And these were only three-foot waves!

A bunch of salty water went up my nose. It

tasted disgusting. I love the taste of fresh snow, but fresh ocean is just plain gross—ugh! I stood up and got back on the green giant. Then I started paddling again. Getting knocked off the board scared me a little bit. Still, I knew I could handle this. I mean, I've won forty-six snowboarding races!

More white foam came down at me. I fell off the board again and even more water went up my nose. Before I had the chance to be upset, I felt a tug at my leg. Was something attacking me? I turned around as fast as I could. I prepared myself for a face-to-face encounter with a great white shark. All I saw, though, was the great green board trying to float back to shore. The leash around my ankle held it back. That was the tug.

I stood in the water for a moment and collected myself. At least I was warmer now. Mrs. Blossom said that my wetsuit would be cold until my skin warmed up. She was right. "Come on Cece, this is easy," I said to myself. Once again, I climbed up and started paddling. Once again, more whitewater came rushing toward me. This time, though, I put my arms down at the end of the board. I put my head down too, closing my eyes as water crashed over me. When I opened my eyes I was still on my board. Ha! I knew I was going to be good at this!

I paddled out a few more strokes to the small waves. I was surprised how much lighter the green giant was in the water. It was pretty easy to move around, too. I finally arrived at the spot where the waves were forming. Right when I got there, I spotted a nice wave in the distance. I paddled to try and catch it. By the time I made it there, the wave was gone. Another wave was forming back where I had just been. I felt like the ocean was playing keep-away from me. I swam back to my first spot, and missed another wave.

"Don't go out too far!" cried a voice that scared me.

I looked to the shore and saw Pam. She was yelling at me through a megaphone. Pam was not someone to be ignored. So I stayed put and hoped that some waves would come my way. I didn't have to wait very long. A small wave came towards me. Quickly, I turned the board around and started paddling. But I soon felt the wave go right under me, without me on it.

I turned away from the shore to watch for another wave. A few seconds later, I was paddling like crazy again. And again I felt the wave pass under me. I didn't know what I was doing wrong. I simply couldn't figure it out.

The rest of the class was catching wave after wave. I watched the boy with the blue eyes. He carved beautiful turns in the ocean. He made it look so easy.

I hated to admit it, but even Portia was pretty good. How could she do this and I couldn't? It didn't make any sense. Didn't the ocean know how good I was at snowboarding?

I decided that there had to be something wrong with my board. That thought led me to smile. Yup, that's all this is— my board is broken. I looked over to Mrs. Blossom. I wanted to let her know about my board. She was on a wave. I didn't want to interrupt her so I decided that I'd keep trying.

"Aloha from the ocean," said a voice from out of nowhere.

I turned around. "Hershel, you scared me."

"My apologies," said Hershel. He looked like a superhero in his bright blue wetsuit. "I just wanted to see how things were going with you."

"It's going okay, I guess. I'm having a little trouble with the board, though. I think it might be broken."

Hershel started laughing pretty hard. "A broken foam board? That is excellent, Cece. Very funny."

"What do you mean?" I asked without a smile.

Hershel stopped laughing. "You mean you're not kidding?"

"Why would I be kidding?"

"Well, that piece of foam is unbreakable." Hershel talked quickly, as usual. "Your board is just fine. Anyway, you think you're ready to try some bigger waves?" asked Hershel.

"No thanks," I said. "I want to get really good at these small ones first."

"Excellent plan. Well, until our paths cross again, I bid you farewell."

"Bye."

I watched Hershel swim back to the crowd. Now that I was alone, I was crying. Who was I fooling? I was no good at surfing. The only thing I was good at was snowboarding. I had no business being in the ocean. I belonged on a mountain. I belonged in Wyoming, not Los Angeles.

In the middle of this thought, I felt something hit me hard in the shoulder. I fell off my board and somersaulted underwater. I swallowed a whole bunch of water before I could get back to the surface. I coughed when my head came up. I tried to stand, but the water was too deep. And it was hard to swim because my leg was tangled on something.

"Grab this." I heard a voice say. My surfboard was now in front of me. I grabbed it. "Are you okay?" the voice asked.

I turned around. There he was—the boy with the blue eyes. "Uhh, yeah," was all I could manage to say.

"I yelled, but I guess you didn't hear me," he said.

"Sorry," I said. "Are you okay?"

"I'm fine," he said, smiling. "I've had much bigger collisions than that."

"I'm sorry for being in your way."

"No worries," he said and smiled again. He had such a nice smile. I was too embarrassed to smile back. He laughed.

"It looks like are leashes are tangled up."

In a flash, Pam the Lifeguard swam up to us with a red floating thing. "Is anyone hurt?"

"No," he told her.

"And I'm fine," I said.

"There's always the possibility of a concussion, though. Here," Pam got on back of the green giant. She motioned for us to get on. "I want to check you both out." Pam paddled us back to shore while the surfing class stared. I wanted to disappear.

Pam made sure that we weren't hurt. The boy with the blue eyes went back out a moment later. I was done for the day. I waited on the shore for the rest of the class to finish. I was beyond embarrassed. I sat on the sand and stared down the shore.

"You stay away from him." Suddenly, I was brought back to reality. Portia was standing above me, her hands on her hips.

"What are you talking about?" I asked.

"Don't play stupid, Wyoming. Jake is mine."

"What? Who's Jake?"

"Boy, you really are dumb. Everyone knows who Jake is. He's only the hottest boy in school. And . . . " Portia leaned into me, "he's my boyfriend."

Jake is the boy with the blue eyes—and he's Portia's boyfriend. Perfect.

"I'll stay away from him," I said. It wouldn't be a problem avoiding Jake because I was never going to surf again.

CHAPTER TWELVE

LOST

When I got home from surfing, I ran straight to my room. Still wearing my wet bathing suit, I called Sally. We talked for a few minutes and I felt a little better. I told her that I wasn't a good surfer. I told her about Portia, that Portia was pure evil. I told her about the boy with the blue eyes and about Hershel, too. She listened to everything. Then she told me that it was going to take time before I became a professional surfer. I laughed. Sally always had a way of making me feel better.

When I hung up with Sally, I tried to find my dad. I needed to talk. I found him in our living room, asleep on the couch. I was bored and lonely, so I decided to call Mom. Since we had moved to LA, I had barely spoken to her. I was mad at Mom for staying behind. Didn't she love me? Didn't she love Dad?

Was her job *that* important?

She answered the phone on the first ring. She sounded really excited to hear from me. I told her a little bit about Los Angeles and my new school. For some reason, though, I put a positive spin on my life in California. I simply couldn't tell her the truth.

I *wanted* to tell her all about my failed attempt at becoming a surfer. I *wanted* to cry to her about the mean kids at David Hasselhoff. Instead, we talked about the Los Angeles weather and the pool in our backyard. I didn't want her to know how unhappy I was. If I could make it seem great in LA, maybe she would join us sooner.

After I hung up, I got into bed early, trying hard to forget the disappointing day. Even with all of my stuff unpacked, my room still seemed empty. I felt empty, too.

I walked up to my bookcase. On the top shelf, I had arranged my favorite snowboarding awards. I looked up at the awards. The most important trophy read: Mount Blizzard Snowboarding Championship, Second Place, Cece Morgan

It's the only second-place medal I ever kept. That's because the Mount Blizzard Championship is the biggest snowboarding competition in Wyoming. Just to compete in it, you have to win at least four other local events.

In my first year of competing, I was second out of the best snowboarders in the state. I reached up and grabbed the Mount Blizzard trophy. It was heavy and felt cool against my skin. I remember standing there during the awards ceremony. As they handed the winner's trophy out, I was sure I would win the next year. That was before I found out that I would be moving to southern California. I sighed and put the trophy back on the shelf. Then I crawled into bed and fell asleep.

I had the strangest dream that night: I was back in Rockville. It had just dumped about two feet of fresh powder. I was on the chairlift riding over one of my favorite runs, Bandits' Getaway. It was still snowing heavily, but it was sunny. The snowflakes reflected little rainbows as they fell down to the ground.

I got off at the top of the lift and sat down in the snow to attach my binding. That's when I noticed that there wasn't any binding. There wasn't even a snowboard attached to my legs. I was on a surfboard. Not a big surfboard like the green giant, but a smaller one.

The next thing I knew, I was flying down Bandits' Getaway. I made long, beautiful turns in the powder. Effortlessly and silently, I made my way down the run. I was at home on the mountain, but I was on a surfboard.

I looked down at the board again. Suddenly, I realized that this shouldn't be happening. I should not be surfing down a mountain! I could not be surfing down a mountain! This was all wrong! And that's when

I lost it. Suddenly the surfboard came to a dead stop in the snow. I flew off the board. Because I was moving so fast, I was launched pretty high. I was about to do a huge face-plant when I woke up.

After a dream like that, I figured I *needed* to go snowboarding. I told my dad that I wanted to try out Big Bison over the weekend.

"Chili, that's three hours away."

"Well, we better leave early then," I said, with determination in my voice.

Dad looked like he was going to say something. I could tell that he wanted to try and talk me out of it. When he looked into my eyes, though, he knew I was going snowboarding. He was driving. I was due that much.

"Sounds like a plan," he said.

I woke him at five on Saturday morning. "Come on, Dad, it's time to go." I said, shaking him. He slowly opened his eyes. Then I turned on his radio full blast. His eyes opened widely. "Well, I'm up now. Thank you, Chili," he mumbled sarcastically. "You sure you want to do this today?" he asked after a huge yawn.

"Of course I'm sure. I want to get there right when it opens."

Twenty minutes later, we were loading up the car. It felt great to unpack my snowboard gear. Oscar wanted to come, but we had to leave him home. "We'll be back soon, boy," I said, scratching his ears.

The ride up took forever. Most of the time we

didn't talk. I didn't have much to say. I didn't like school, I wasn't good at surfing, I sort of had one friend. It was all stuff I didn't feel like talking about.

My dad's show was doing really well. He was having a great time and everyone seemed to like him. That was the good news. I didn't really want to talk about that either. Secretly, I was hoping his show would tank and we would have to move back to Wyoming. That scenario was looking less and less likely.

We'd been in Los Angeles for three weeks and my mom still hadn't come out. Every week, she had to work on some important project. There was always something. I definitely didn't want to talk about that.

So, instead of talking, I looked out the window. It took about two hours to get into the less populated areas. We'd pass a small town, and then there'd be wilderness. I started to feel at home. I wondered when we were going to start seeing snow. Then the road started to get curvy, which I thought was a good sign. I stared out the window looking for any sign of snow. I still didn't see any and I was starting to get worried. How could there be a ski resort if there wasn't any snow?

We eventually came to a sign that read: Big Bison—Next Right. And a moment later, we pulled into a huge gravel parking lot. The mountain didn't open for another half-hour, but the parking lot was already full.

I couldn't understand how there was snow on the mountain but none in the lot. We walked up to the ticket booth. At the booth, I asked the cashier how there was snow on the mountain.

"Snowmakers," said the cashier.

"Excuse me?" I asked.

"We've got the most sophisticated snow-making machines. Some people say it's better than real snow." I soon realized that the people who said this were idiots. The fake stuff wasn't even half as good as real snow. After I had taken my first run, I was totally disappointed. Sure, it was awesome to be snowboarding again. But still, this wasn't the same sport I had grown to love back home.

I got off the chairlift after my first run and stood on my board daydreaming. Even under these conditions, snowboarding is the best sport in the world. I continued this thought: surfing is probably the second best sport. I was surprised by that last thought. Did I really like surfing that much? I rolled this thought around for a moment. Yeah, I guess I did. I just wasn't any good at it. I shook these strange thoughts from my head and got ready for my next run.

I slid over to a spot where I could put on my binding. It felt great to just be on my board again. I strapped in and headed down the mountain for my second run. The first fifty yards or so were okay. I started to pick up some speed, but it was difficult. I had to navigate in between several other less experienced snowboarders. What was worse, the surface was awful. My board didn't move the way it did back home. The fake snow was somehow stickier than the Rockville snow I was used to. It held on to my board and made my run slower.

Everything looked strange, too. I didn't see giant pine trees covered in snow. In their place were bad snowboarders and a whole bunch of snowmaking machines. I headed closer to the huge machines, in search of better snow.

Unfortunately, the snow wasn't any better by the machines. It was a little deeper, yes, but it was still sticky. Plus, the machine spat out chunks of ice every so often. So I moved back to the middle, where the skiers and snowboarders were. A minute later, I finished that run and went back on the chairlift for another.

My next run felt pretty good—at first. For a moment, I even forgot where I was. I forgot about the lines and the people everywhere, too. I pretended to be back home in Rockville and it worked for a bit.

Then I started to notice that the mountain was really filling up. I couldn't believe how many people had arrived since I had. People were falling in front of me and turning right into me every few seconds. My board scraped over a rock that I couldn't see poking out of the ground. I pictured the huge, ugly, scratch it must have made.

When I got to the bottom of my fourth run, I

pulled off my goggles. I was through. I looked up and noticed that the line for the chairlift was even longer than before. Yup, I was done with Big Bison.

I found my dad in the lodge reading a book. "I'm ready to go home now," I told him.

My dad looked surprised to see me. "But we just got here an hour ago."

"Well, I'm not snowboarding anymore," I told him. My lip started trembling and I nearly started to cry—again.

"Hey, it's okay, Chili, we can go home." My dad reached out and touched me on the shoulder. "What happened?" he asked.

"Nothing, it's just not like snowboarding at home. Three-hour drive, long lines— I just think. . ." I paused, not sure what I really wanted to say. "It's just too frustrating, Dad. It makes me miss home too much." I took a deep breath. "Thanks for trying. This place doesn't make me feel good." I spoke sadly.

When we loaded up my snowboard, I saw two big scratches from the rocks. I was quiet all the way home.

CHAPTER THIRTEEN

BAD TO WORSE

On the Monday after my visit to Big Bison, school was not much fun. It seemed like all of the energy had been sucked out of me. Snowboarding in California was not like snowboarding in Wyoming. I was an athlete without a sport.

Mrs. Blossom was alone when I walked into her first period class. "Hey Cece." She didn't waste any time, "are we going to see you at Surf Club on Wednesday?"

I could feel my heart beating through my chest. "Oh, I don't know if I can make it on Friday. There's a lot of stuff that my dad and I have to take care of. You know." I had no idea what I was talking about.

She leaned in close to me. "Can I tell you a secret?"

"Sure."

"I used to be one of the worst surfers ever."

"You?" I asked. I couldn't picture Mrs. Blossom being bad at surfing. It seemed like she was born to it.

"Oh, I was a joke in the water. It took me three months before I stood up for the first time. And that was with surfing every day!"

"Wow." That's a long time to be horrible at something. "Why did you keep doing it?" I asked.

"I loved being in the water. It didn't matter that I wasn't getting better. I was just happy to be there."

I didn't really understand the point of doing something that you weren't good at.

"Is there any chance we'll see you at Surf Club on Friday? After you and your dad take care things?" Mrs. Blossom winked at me.

She had me cornered. "We'll see," I said. "Things really have been busy with us getting settled in the house." I didn't know what else to say. I knew that deep down I liked the sport of surfing. But I also knew that I didn't want to embarrass myself again.

Hershel walked in and saved me. "Excellent morning to you, Cece—and excellent morning to you, Mrs. Blossom." I smiled at the sight of my only friend in Los Angeles.

"Morning, Hershel," said Mrs. Blossom.

The class began to fill up. Mrs. Blossom moved to the front of the room. "Take your seats, please—we've got a lot to cover today."

We sat down. I hadn't realized it, but Portia was already there. She looked at me from across the room. Oh, how I dreaded and disliked her.

In the middle of Mrs. Blossom's lesson, I felt a tap on my shoulder. I turned around. A boy behind me handed me a note, folded into a neat rectangle. The outside was marked in red pen: For stupid Cece. I opened up the note and in the same red pen it read: Stay away from Jake, stupid!

It didn't take a genius to figure out that the note was from Portia. Who else would be that mean? I looked over at her and she glared back. I tried to ignore her for the rest of class. The bell rang. I waited for Portia to leave before I left. Hershel was nice enough to wait with me.

When we got to the hallway, Portia was standing next to Jake. She was acting all nice and sweet to him. I didn't get it. Jake seemed like such a good guy. Didn't he see how horrid Portia was? Didn't he care how mean she was? Portia noticed me staring at her and flashed me an evil grin. Then she put her arm around Jake. He smiled. Couldn't *something* go my way, just once? I wondered.

How come when bad stuff happens, it always happens all at once? I was horrible at surfing, snowboarding in California was terrible. Plus, the boy I liked was dating the girl I hated. That should have been enough bad stuff for a while, right? Well, all of that combined wasn't as bad as this...

"Hey, Cece," Dad said flatly. "How was school?" *Uh, oh, he called me Cece.* The only time my dad ever called me Cece was when something was wrong. Dad tried to smile, but I could tell he was faking it.

"What's wrong?" I asked, with a look of panic on my face.

"Umm, well, I don't really know how to say this, Cece." Dad fidgeted a bit in the driver's seat. I leaned up. "I was going to wait until we got home." He looked into my eyes. "Your mother called this morning."

"Okay," I was waiting. "So what?"

Dad swallowed hard. "Well, she thinks it might be best if she stays in Wyoming for a while."

"What do you mean, a while?" I asked. "Like a month or two?" This did not sound good.

"I'm not really sure, Cece."

"Are you guys getting a divorce or something?" I was fairly certain—I sure hoped—that I was jumping to a silly conclusion. My parents couldn't get divorced. They loved each other. Didn't they?

Dad paused for a moment. He had a funny look on his face. "I don't know," he said, almost whispering.

"What do you mean you don't know?" I screamed. "How could you not know?" This terrible scenario made my stomach turn.

"Your mother can't leave her job right now. And she's not thrilled about moving to Los Angeles."

Now I couldn't hold back my tears. They started pouring out. "Well, neither was I, but I still had to come out here!"

My dad pulled over to the side of the road. "Honey, I'm sorry," he said. He reached over to give me a hug. "Everything is going to work out."

"Don't touch me!" I screamed at him. "How can you guys do this to me? I hate you both!"

Dad tried to calm me down. "Come on Chili, what do you say we get some ice cream over at . . ."

I cut him off. "Don't talk to me! Just take me home!" I yelled, before putting my head in my hands and sobbing.

The moment we got home, I grabbed Oscar and went up to my room. It felt even emptier than before. I immediately buried my face in my pillow. I barely heard Dad tapping at my door a few minutes later. "Can I come in, Cece?"

I didn't feel like answering. I didn't feel like moving.

A few seconds later, I felt him sit down on my bed. "Cece, can you please pick up your head? We need to talk."

"No." My voice was muffled coming through the pillow.

"Will you look at me?" Even through the pillow, I could hear the sadness in my dad's voice. Still,

I wasn't moving. It was quiet for a few seconds. "Neither your mom nor I are happy about this . . . "

Then why are you doing it, I wondered.

"The fact is, though, we've been having some problems for a while now." He paused for a second. "We need to spend some time apart. This would have happened even if we were still in Wyoming."

Yeah, right, I thought.

"I want to be honest with you as best I can, Cece. And honestly, I don't know what's going to happen. I don't know if we're going to get back together or." He paused again. I could hear him sniffle. Was he crying? "This may be permanent. We don't know. But your mother and I love you very much. This has nothing to do with you. I'm so sorry, Chili."

I didn't move.

My dad sniffed again and coughed. "Is there anything you want to say? Anything at all?"

I still didn't move.

I felt his weight rise off my bed. "Well, whenever you want to talk, I'm here. Sometimes talking about stuff makes you feel better. I could use someone to talk to. I love you."

I wanted to reach out and hug him to make him feel better. I wanted to sit down and figure out where he and Mom went wrong. But I just couldn't do these things. I was too upset.

CHAPTER FOURTEEN

WAKING UP

I have never walked in my sleep before. Still, I felt like that was what I was doing over the next couple of weeks. All this stuff was happening around me, but I just plodded along, with no emotions.

I couldn't feel anything. I wasn't happy or sad or even hungry. I wasn't anything. School, Portia, Dad, Mom, surfing, Jake, Hershel, and even Oscar—none of it affected me.

My dad kept trying to talk to me, but I wasn't listening. I mean, the thought "my parents are going to get divorced" was definitely in my head. It just didn't connect to anything. It bounced around like a pinball. I couldn't make it mean anything.

On the one-month anniversary of my time in LA, Oscar woke me up early. I petted him and looked at the clock. It was 5:14 in the morning. The past few weeks had been absolute misery. I barely spoke to anyone—not even Sally.

"Come on Oscar, it's not time to get up yet." I tried to make him go back to sleep, but he wasn't having any of it. He was wide awake. "Do you need to go out?"

Oscar wagged his tail, which means yes. He then spun around in circles, just like he always did when he got excited. "Okay, okay! Shhhh." I stretched and rubbed my eyes. Then I climbed out of bed and made my way downstairs. The house was quiet. I opened the door for Oscar to go outside, but he just stood there. "What's the matter, boy?" I asked.

Oscar looked outside, then back at me. He didn't move. "Come on, go outside," I said, motioning to the open door. Oscar sat down. What was wrong with him? "Don't you want to go out?" I asked. He looked up again, cocking his head and smiling. I didn't get it. As I took a step towards the door to close it, Oscar barked.

"What?" I asked him.

Oscar kept smiling and wagged his tail. He sure was acting weird this morning.

I opened the door again, but this time I stepped outside. A flash of gray shot out in front of me. Suddenly, Oscar was running around the yard like a crazy dog. I laughed for the first time in a while.

Oscar came up to me with his tongue hanging out of his mouth. I looked down at him, and then up at the sky. It was mostly dark, but there was a hint of pink on the horizon. Everything was quiet. At five in the morning, it was hard to tell Los Angeles was a gigantic, crowded, horrible city. It was actually pretty nice.

Suddenly, Oscar stood up and ran towards the pool. He barked at me to follow him, so I did. We stood at the edge of the pool. Without warning, there was a splash as Oscar jumped into the pool. I laughed, "Oscar, what are you doing, boy?"

He paddled around like he was in heaven. He was having a great time. Then he swam up to where I was standing. He barked, asking me to come in. It did look like fun in there, but it was so early. Oscar barked again.

"Okay," I said. "You know, you really are a crazy dog. Wait a second." I ran into the house and up the stairs, quickly throwing on my bathing suit. I ran back downstairs and jumped in the pool. The water was perfect. The moment I hit that water something changed inside of me. I felt awake for the first time in weeks. Oscar swam up to me. I pet his soggy head. "Thanks, Oscar," I said. He barked and we played in the water some more.

"What are you doing?" My dad was standing on the patio wearing his shaggy white robe.

"Just taking a swim," I said.

"Oh," said my dad. He looked at Oscar and me in the pool. We were both smiling. "Can I come in?"

"Sure." I said.

The next thing I knew Dad had jumped into the water. The three of us swam around for the next thirty minutes. It was probably the most fun I'd had since we moved to California. I thought about the people I knew back home in Rockville. I thought about how excited they would be to take a swim at five o'clock in the morning.

After that swim, something inside of me was knocked back into place. I had finally accepted my fate: I was in Los Angeles, for better or for worse. There was no reason to fight it anymore. My parents weren't living together. They might even get divorced. Sally was a thousand miles away. Big Bison was a disaster area. Jake was dating Portia. There was nothing I could do to change any of these things. I decided to stop letting things that I couldn't control make me sad. It was time that I took my life into my own hands. It was up to me to make myself happy again.

That morning, I went up to Mrs. Blossom's desk after class. She had a stack of papers in front of her. "Mrs. Blossom?"

She looked up at me. "Hi, Cece." She slid the paper to the side. "What's up?"

"I'd like to go out with the Surfing Club again."

Mrs. Blossom smiled. "That's great, Cece! You're always welcome. I'm so glad you're coming out with us!" She clapped her hands and gave me an excited hug. Mrs. Blossom was the best. "The waves are going to be awesome today," she predicted.

"Cool," I said. "Well, I'll see you later then." I headed out of the room.

"Cece?"

I turned around. "Yes?"

"It's fun to just be in the water."

I didn't exactly know how to respond. "Okay," was all I said.

CHAPTER FIFTEEN

STANDING UP

So, there I was with the green board attached to my ankle. I stood at the shore watching the waves. I wasn't quite ready to go in yet.

Foamy water rushed up and met my feet. It was cold, but it felt good. I took a few steps into the ocean. Once I was up to my knees, I got on top of the green giant and paddled. I arrived at a spot where small waves were forming. I sat there, trying to see a pattern. If there was one, I couldn't see it.

I sat for a few minutes, bobbing up and down. I couldn't get over how hot it was out here. Especially since Sally had told me that it was still snowing back home!

Just then, I noticed a wave approaching. I quickly turned and started paddling as fast as I could. I dug my arms deep into the water like Hershel told me to.

As I dug my arms deeper, I could feel the board moving faster. I kept paddling. The wave approached. I kept paddling. Then I felt the wave pick me up. For a second or two, I was actually riding along with the wave. It was awesome! I was going so fast—I could really feel the power of the wave beneath me. My heart sped up in excitement. I kept paddling. Then, the wave passed underneath me. The water curled over without me inside. "That was close," I said to no one in particular.

I turned back around and watched for more waves to come. I was determined now. I wanted the feeling I had just experienced to come again and again. A few more waves came through and I tried to ride each of them. It seemed like I was getting closer to actually standing up. I was finally getting the feel of it.

I caught some waves for a few seconds, but not long enough to stand. The last wave that I caught was the best. This one actually crashed with me in it, and it was amazing. But when it was time to stand up, I was too scared. I was sure that if I stood, I would crash. So I held onto the board tightly and rode the wave in.

I paddled back out past the break after that ride. I wanted another chance. During the next few minutes, my spot was pretty calm. I was lying down on my board, listening to the sounds of the ocean. The gentle splashing of the water over the front of the green giant was soothing. I thought about what Mrs. Blossom said earlier. It's fun just to be out here. I smiled. She was right.

Then I froze. About twenty feet off to my right, I saw a pair of fins. The kind of fins that belong to an animal that could eat me! I was too scared to do anything. I couldn't yell. I couldn't swim away. All I could do was watch in horror as the fins moved closer. Nobody told me that there were really sharks in the ocean!

The sharks kept swimming closer. I could see water shooting out from their blowholes. Wait a minute, sharks don't have blowholes. Dolphins have blowholes. I looked closer at the pair of fins. Their shiny skin reflected brightly in the sun. One of the fins disappeared underwater for a second. Then it came up and water shot out from the top of its head.

I relaxed when I was certain that these were dolphins, not sharks. They swam up pretty close to me. Not close enough to touch, but close enough to see their faces. They were awesome looking. As they sliced through the water, I could see them smiling.

I watched the dolphins swim away. I watched until I couldn't see their fins any more. It was amazing! I felt truly happy. I wasn't even upset when the time arrived to go home. I hadn't stood on my board yet, but I was getting close.

The next day at school, Hershel came up to me in the cafeteria. He was acting even more excited than usual. "Hello, my friend," he said. "I have excellent news."

"What's that?" I asked.

Hershel picked up his grilled cheese and avocado sandwich. He took a bite and chewed slowly. He swallowed and then took a sip of milk.

"Come on already, Hershel," I said, losing patience.

Hershel wiped off the milk moustache from his upper lip. "This is secret information, so don't go spreading it. Mrs. Blossom entered the Surfing Club in the Super Wave Junior Championships."

"How do you know? Mrs. Blossom told you?" I asked.

Hershel nodded.

"How is it a secret if she told you?" I asked.

Hershel looked down. "I like secret information," he said. I quickly realized that this piece of news was hardly a secret.

"Can you tell me any more about the competition?" I asked. "Or is that a secret too?"

"I guess I can tell you," said Hershel. He leaned in closer. "Mrs. Blossom said that the competition is one month from this coming Saturday. It's going to be held at Dolly Parton State Park. Eleven other schools will be competing." Hershel moved his eyes back and forth to make sure that no one was listening. "That's all the information I can give you at this time."

I thought about the tournament. I was sure my days of competing were over after I left Rockville for Los Angeles. But I really did like surfing. If I took a month to practice, maybe I would get better. After all, I'd gotten close to standing up yesterday.

I was deep in thought when I was interrupted: "Well, isn't this just the cutest pair of dorks you could ever hope to meet?"

There was only one person whose voice could sound so mean. "What do you want?" I asked coldly. I lifted my head and saw Portia surrounded by a few of her friends.

"I heard that Mrs. Blossom entered us in a tournament," said Portia.

I looked at Hershel. "Some secret," I whispered.

Hershel flashed an embarrassed grin.

"We're here to make sure that you don't enter the competition," Portia said. "Everyone knows how bad you are, Cece. You can't embarrass our school. We have a reputation that we don't want ruined by some small town loser."

Her little group of clones laughed and nodded. But something was different today. I wasn't going to sit back and let life happen to me any more. I was going to *make* things happen. Portia had made me sad. Now she was making me mad—really mad. And now I had the courage to do something about it. "Why do you spend so much of your time worried about me?" I stood up and faced Portia. "Don't you think you're pretty lame?"

"What did you just say to me?" she asked, a little angrily. She was clearly surprised. I don't think very many people had spoken to her like this.

Hershel looked stunned by my aggressive response to Portia. He put his hand on my shoulder. "Maybe you should sit down and . . ."

"I got this Hershel." I shoved his hand off my shoulder. Then I looked at Portia again. "You walk around like you own this school. Well, you don't! There are more of us losers than there are of you." A small crowd started to gather around us. "I think it's time that we start standing up for ourselves." A few people in the crowd cheered. "You hear that?" I said. "We're not going to take it from you anymore. Do you know why?"

Portia looked different than I had ever seen her before. Her face was bright red. She looked scared. "Why?" she asked.

"Because I know the truth about you." I said.

"Oh yeah, and what's that?" Portia asked.

"You're a scared little girl who hides behind her meanness." I moved even closer to her. "I know, Portia, that you are jealous of us losers who *are* something."

"Me, jealous of you?" Portia laughed, but a little nervously.

"That's right," I said. Portia backed away from me a few steps. I continued. "I feel sorry for you. You might be popular, but I would never trade places with you. I like being something, even if it's a hick from Wyoming."

Portia let out a little gasp to respond, but nothing came out. There was more cheering and laughing from the growing crowd.

I kept talking. "So let me tell you what's next: you're going to leave me alone. I'm going to enter that surfing competition, too. And there's nothing you can do about it."

Portia didn't speak. One of her friends whispered something in her ear. Then Portia started to speak, "Listen, Wyoming freak . . ."

"Shut up. I am not a freak. You will never call me that again. Got it?"

She didn't say anything.

I shouted at her. "I asked you a question! Do you understand?"

"Yes," she whispered.

"Good, then get out of my face and stay out of my way."

Portia looked like she was about to cry. She turned and walked away. I sat back down in my seat. I had never spoken to anyone that way before.

"Wow, Cece! That was unbelievable, amazing—it was excellent!" said Hershel. "I had no idea you were so tough!" Hershel wore a large grin on his face. The grin quickly turned into a more serious expression. "We've got some work to do, though, tough girl. We need to get you ready for the competition."

CHAPTER SIXTEEN

JUST DO IT

The next morning I was nervous about school. I didn't know what Portia was going to do. As Mrs. Blossom began talking during first period, I glanced around the room. I saw Portia and expected her to attack me. When she noticed me looking, though, she avoided my eyes. I kept staring at her. She just sat there slumped in her chair. She looked a little like I felt after one of her attacks.

I didn't think it was possible for her to feel those feelings. I never thought of someone like her having feelings. But looking at her there, I knew that she definitely did. Even after all she put me through I felt sorry for her.

As the day wore on, I began to feel more comfortable. People say that the way to deal with bullies is to stand up to them. I guess they're right.

That night, the phone rang while my dad and I were eating dinner.

I got up from the table to answer it. "Hello," I said.

"Cece?"

"Sally!"

"I finally found you! Where have you been?" she asked.

"I've been hiding out." I sighed. "I've been pretty sad."

"I called you like . . ."

"I know," I said, "can we just forget it, Sally?"

"Sure." She paused. "You sound weird, Cece."

"Well, I'm eating a burrito, plus, I just fixed my entire life. Everything is going to be fine now."

"I never knew anything wasn't going to be fine. Are you sure you're okay?"

"I am excellent, Sally." I said, stealing Hershel's favorite word.

"You sound like you've had one too many burritos."

I laughed I was excited to hear her voice.

"Can you talk?" she asked.

"Sure," I said, walking into our living room.

"Cool," said Sally. "Well, see, my mom ran into your mom." I knew where this was going. I hadn't told Sally about my parents splitting up. "Your mom told my mom that she's not moving to Los Angeles."

I didn't know exactly what to say. "That's true,"

was all I said.

"Why didn't you tell me?" asked Sally. I could hear a little bit of hurt in her voice.

"I don't know. I guess I didn't want it to be true. Once I tell you, then it's real, you know?"

"Oh," said Sally. "Well, do you want to tell me about it now?"

I still didn't feel like talking about it. I was getting by pretending that nothing was really wrong. I started getting a little choked up. "I don't think I'm ready yet, Sally."

She could tell I was getting upset. "That's okay, Cece, we don't have to talk about it. Whenever you want to, though, you know I'm here, right?"

"Yes," I said. I did know she was there, but it was still nice to hear. "Thank you."

"You don't have to thank me," said Sally. "That's what friends do." I smiled. "You know what else friends do?" she asked.

"What's that?"

"They come visit their friends in Los Angeles."

I screamed, "Are you kidding? When?"

"In a month! We have break at the same time. I'm coming for a whole week! I already have my plane ticket and everything."

This was the best news ever! "We are going to have such a good time. I can't wait!" I said excitedly.

"I can't wait either," Sally said. "And, Cece, if you want to talk about anything beforehand, you can, okay?"

"Thanks, Sally," I said. I don't think there's a better friend in the world than Sally.

After I hung up, I realized Sally would be visiting during the Super Wave Junior Championships. Now I really needed to do well. Sally has only seen me win.

That night, I took out my Three Special Things from my nightstand drawer. I held the ceramic orange in my hand first. I looked closely at the glossy skin. The top layer was clear and clean.

I put on Mom's glasses next. The room turned fuzzy as I looked through the thick lenses. I looked over at my bookcase and the trophies on the top shelf. All of my awards looked like one big shiny blob. I smiled at Oscar. Then I heard a noise by the door and quickly took the glasses off. "What are you doing in here, Dad?"

"Your door was open," he said. "I just wanted to say goodnight." He walked over to my nightstand. "Where'd you get that?" he asked, holding up the picture of him and my mother. He took a long look at it.

"I've had it for a long time," I confessed. "Can you please put it down?" I could feel my face turning red. No one but Oscar knew about my Three Special Things. I wanted to keep it that way. My dad kept standing there, though. He kept starting at the picture. His eyes welled up with tears.

"Dad?"

"Yes, Chili?"

"Can you please get out?" He was making me uncomfortable. He just kept looking at the picture.

"Sure, sweetheart," said my dad. He put the frame back on my nightstand and turned around to leave. He looked sad.

"Wait, Dad." I stopped him. I felt really bad for him.

"Yeah, Chili."

"When you and Mom got married," I said, then paused. "Did you ever think . . ."

He finished my sentence. "That we wouldn't stay married? Not a chance." He picked up the pic ture again and looked at it. "I thought we would be like this forever."

I swallowed hard so I could speak. I was finally ready to talk about this. "So what happened?" My dad sat down on my bed. I sat next to him. "Your mother and I really loved each other a lot when we got married." He paused, "The truth is, Chili, she's the only woman I've ever loved."

I sighed. "It sounds like you're reading an anniversary card or something."

"Wait a second, it gets more interesting." He sighed. "Eventually, your mom and I started getting really into our jobs. We were both extremely motivated. We wanted to be successful. We started working more and more. We spent less and less time talking to each other. I'm not sure if either one of us even noticed that it happened, Chili." Dad moved some hair away from my face. "Watching you grow up kept us together. We both love you so much—so we stuck it out. But during these past few years, it's gotten worse. Your Mom and I have barely been speaking to each other." Dad's lower lip began to shake, "I never wanted to live apart from your mom, but . . ."

I could tell that Dad was about to cry. So before he could continue talking, I gave him a hug. "I just want you both to be happy. I don't want to make things harder on you guys. If you need to be apart, that's okay with me. You don't have to stick together for me."

After I finished talking, Dad squeezed me. "We're gonna be great. Everything is going to be great, Chili. And just so you know—I will always love your mother. She's the reason you're alive, and you're the greatest thing I have."

"Thanks, Dad." I smiled. "You're cool too." I held up my mom's glasses, "One more question: why does Mom have paint all over her glasses?" I handed them to him.

He held them in his hands and smiled. "Well, before she started working, she would paint every day. You don't remember that?"

"No, I don't think I've ever seen Mom paint."

"I guess you were just a baby. Well, you're lucky. She was absolutely horrible." He laughed.

"What kind of stuff did she paint?" I asked, smiling.

"She painted everything—landscapes, portraits." My dad laughed out loud. "She was probably the worst painter ever."

"Why did she paint so much then?"

"She loved it. It didn't matter to her that her paintings were ugly. She was the first person to admit that she wasn't any good." My dad looked at me and grinned. "That's your mom, for you. You remind me of her sometimes, Chili." He kissed me on the top of my head. "Anyway, goodnight."

"Goodnight." I said.

I knew right then that Mom would enter the surfing competition no matter how bad she was. I looked at her glasses again. Then, I put my Three Special Things back in my drawer.

Without even thinking, I picked up the phone and called Mom. I knew it was late in Rockville, but I didn't care. We talked for over an hour. It felt so good to talk to her. I told her all about Los Angeles. This time, I didn't leave out the important details. I told her that Dad had told me about her paintings. She laughed at that. We talked about her and Dad, too. She said a lot of the same things he had.

I decided that I was going to have to let that be. I reminded myself not to get upset about things I couldn't control. If they didn't want to stay married, I wasn't going to get in the way. It was going to take some adjusting, though. I told Mom this and she started to cry. By the end of the conversation, Mom and I had a plan set for me to visit Rockville. She promised to take the week off. I would be able to do all the snowboarding I wanted! I couldn't wait.

I said goodnight and snuggled close to Oscar. When I closed my eyes, I realized that I felt happy. Sure, I was sad that my parents were probably not going to get back together. But I was happy because I knew in my heart that they both loved me. It was like a weight had been lifted. Dad was right—sometimes it helps to talk about stuff.

CHAPTER SEVENTEEN

TRAINING

The next morning at school, I needed to talk to Hershel right away. He was busy writing down notes while he measured an old tree out in front of the school.

"Hey, Hershel, can I talk to you for a minute?"

"Absolutely, what can I do for you today?"

"Well, I've been thinking a lot about . . ." I couldn't' finish my sentence. "Wait, what are you recording?"

"I'm measuring the width of the base of this tree. I've been doing it every day since I moved here."

I was about to ask him why, but I didn't. I knew my question would lead into a ten minute lecture. So I left it alone. "Anyway," I said, "this Super Wave Championship thing."

"Yes?" asked Hershel, grinning.

"Well, I'd like to try and not totally embarrass myself."

"Excellent idea."

"Yeah, but I'm a pretty bad surfer," I reminded him.

"You are an inexperienced surfer. That's all. I think you're excellent." What a surprise.

"Thank you, but I am pretty bad." I stared at Hershel's measuring tape, notepad, and pen. "Why do you think of all these funny things to do? Are you bored or something?"

He smiled. "Nope. I'm the opposite of bored. I am so excited by everything that I just can't help doing experiments. I like doing this stuff so I just do it."

Hershel reminded me of what Dad said about Mom. She just wanted to do it, so she did it. That's kind of how I felt about surfing.

"Do you think that you can help me be a better surfer?" I looked back at Hershel.

"I can definitely help you. We can even start today." Hershel smiled.

Four hours later, we were back at Dolly Parton State Park. We suited up and I grabbed the green giant. "I am going to stand on a wave today," I spoke with determination.

Once I reached the water, I dove onto my board. Hershel swam alongside me past the breaking waves.

I stopped paddling when the water was up above Hershel's shoulders.

Finally, the ocean started getting choppy. "Do you see it?" Hershel asked.

"Yes," I said, noticing a wave forming in the distance.

"Then turn around," Hershel spoke forcefully. "Start paddling like crazy!"

I turned around and started paddling.

"Excellent," said Hershel. "Paddle, paddle, paddle. Dig those arms deep in the water." I looked over my shoulder and saw Hershel behind me. He had his hands on the board and was kicking along as I paddled. The wave was coming closer. I kept paddling. "Paddle, paddle, paddle," shouted Hershel behind me.

I felt the wave come up under me. I kept paddling and digging my arms as deep as I could. Hershel let go. The green giant got caught in the wave and started to move—without me paddling. I was in the wave!

"Now jump up!" shouted Hershel.

This was the hard part, but I had to do it. So I pushed my arms down and jumped up to my feet. I nearly fell, but I looked up to realize that I was riding the wave. I was surfing!

"All the way up!" shouted Hershel.

I stood all the way up. "Woohoo!" I couldn't believe it. I was really surfing! The wave was moving me towards the shore. "I'm surfing!" It was beautiful. I was completely weightless, like I was flying. I shifted my weight and turned the board a little to the left. Then I turned the board a little to the right.

The wave kept moving me closer to the shore. I didn't want to crash into the sand so I jumped off the green giant. Cool water rushed over me. My feet touched the soft sandy bottom. I stood up, opened my eyes, and took a breath. I had just ridden my very first wave. Right after I finished that ride, I grabbed my board and raced back out. I was officially hooked.

Hershel swam up to me. "Nice ride," he said.

"That was the coolest thing ever," I flung myself at Hershel and gave him a huge hug. I was so excited. I felt as if I had just won a race. Hershel and I stared at each other for a moment after I let go of him. He looked cute wearing that oversized wetsuit of his. "Thanks, Hershel," I said, quickly turning my head away.

"For what?" asked Hershel.

"I couldn't have gotten up on that wave without you."

"You just needed a little push. The rest was all you."

"Still, thanks."

"My pleasure," Hershel said. "You looked beautiful riding that wave." Now it was him looking away from me. "I mean, you and the wave, with the sun and everything—together—excellent."

CHAPTER EIGHTEEN

SURFER

We rode like that for the rest of the afternoon. After an hour, Hershel went and grabbed his board. I no longer needed his help to get onto a wave. I had the feel down at this point. I quickly realized that surfing wasn't about proving something to Portia either.

It was all about the ride.

Speaking of Portia, she left me alone in the weeks leading up to the championships. It was almost as if I had a Portia Pass. She never apologized for being horrible to me. But still, not having to deal with her was great.

I saw Jake in the halls and at surfing club. I was realizing more and more that he was kind of a jerk too. I saw him give some fifth-grader a wedgie in the hallway outside of art class. All of his friends were laughing and the kid was crying. Jake started to remind me of Portia. I wasn't excited about him anymore

Dad's show was doing great! The country really liked Mad Marty in the Morning. Mom was planning a summer trip out to Los Angeles. I was excited, secretly hoping she and Dad would fall in love again. Oscar, of course, was the world's greatest dog.

During the next few weeks, Hershel and I went surfing as much as we could. He really helped me a lot. Every time we went out, I felt more comfortable in the ocean. I didn't need to use the green giant anymore either. The smaller boards were much harder to surf on, but I kept improving.

Things were going very well until about a week before the event. Once I'd learned how to surf, the competition started to mean more to me. The realization that I would be competing, and *not* winning started to set in.

I tried to explain this to Hershel before we went in the ocean. His response was totally Hershel. "What exactly is so important about winning?"

"What do you mean?" I asked him.

"Why do you feel like you have to win?" Hershel wasn't backing off.

"Isn't that why *you* compete?" I asked

"Not me." Hershel stared up at me, "I surf for the ride. I compete for the heck of it. Don't think that means I'm not excited for the event. I love being around people who enjoy the same things I do. Plus, I plan on recruiting some new members to the Lunar Club."

We paddled into the ocean. It was a beautiful day. The sunlight hit the tops of the waves. I breathed in the clean salty air through my nose and smiled. The waves were much bigger than the ones we usually rode. I watched a big wave break ahead of us.

"Looks like the ocean is a little more excited today," Hershel remarked.

I nodded.

"Do you want to head back to shore?"

I was a bit scared of the giant waves. But something made me not turn around. It was probably Hershel's goofy grin and his giant blue wetsuit. I figured that if *he* could be out in the ocean, then I could too. "No," I said. "Let's keep going."

"Excellent."

We had to paddle out past the breaking waves. This was a challenge because the waves continued to break on top of us. I closed my eyes and pushed the front of my board down. The cool water rushed over me. I popped back up and immediately started paddling. I made it past the breaking point and caught up to Hershel.

"Are you ready to take a ride?" he asked, out of breath.

"I think so." I was ready, but these waves were huge!

"The next good wave is all yours."

I spotted something forming in the distance. I turned around and paddled as hard as I could. I dug my arms deeper into the water. My board started to pick up speed. I could hear the wave growing behind me. My heart was beating fast again, but this time out of excitement. My board rose up as the giant wave made its way to the shore. I could see the lip of the wave forming right in front of me. I could almost predict exactly how this monster would break. I dug as deep and hard as I could into the water. My board got caught in the wave perfectly—right at the top. As fast as I could, I pushed up into a crouch.

The wave was moving really fast, and I was in it. I stood all the way up. I was flying. Once up, I knew exactly what to do. I shifted my weight and made small turns on the wave. I made a few wider turns, too. Even though I was in the ocean, I felt like I was back at home on my snowboard.

I made a bigger turn towards the curl of the wave. This turn was a little too big. The next thing I knew, I was caught in the lip of the wave. Then I was thrown backwards into the ocean. The water stung my back as I hit the deck. It didn't hurt too much, though. The wave crashed over me and I somersaulted a few times underwater.

When I came up, Hershel was right next to me. "That was quite a wipeout. Are you okay?"

"I am most excellent," I said to Hershel. He laughed. I laughed. My grin was almost as big as his.

CHAPTER NINETEEN

THE RIDE

The Super Wave Championship was on Sunday. Sally came into town on Saturday, the day before the event. My dad and I picked her up at the airport. It was so good to see her.

It was Sally's first time to California, and she was a little excited. "I can't believe you guys live here," she said looking out the window. "You guys are so lucky. This place is awesome!" She pointed to her right. "That whole street is bigger than Rockville. Wow. Look at the green hair on that guy. There's the Hollywood sign! It's huge!"

It was good to be with my friend again.

Sally was even more excited when she saw our house. "No way!" she said as we pulled into the driveway. "This is really where you guys live?" I thought she was going to pass out when I showed her the pool. "If I lived here, I would spend every second in the pool," she said. "Cece, this is absolutely amazing. I don't know how you ever didn't like it here. This place is the coolest place in the world!" Sally was just like Hershel, she made you get excited about things.

We stayed up late that night talking and watching movies. It was just like things were back home. We talked about everything, even my parents. I told her that they probably weren't going to get back together. I told her that I was okay with it. She gave me a hug and I cried a little, but I was fine.

The next morning we had to get up really early. The Super Wave Championship started at seven. My dad woke us up at six. I was really tired. After we ate breakfast, we piled into the car and headed for the beach.

There was a small crowd already gathering when we got there. Mrs. Blossom was standing by the judges' booth. The butterflies were already forming in my stomach. This was the first time I'd competed in anything besides snowboarding.

We spotted Hershel. He was hard to miss in his neon green shirt. I noticed that there was a drawing of the moon on the front of his shirt and the words: The lunar club is out of this world. He wasn't kidding about trying to get new members. I introduced him to Sally. She and Hershel talked for a few minutes while I went to fill out some forms.

When I came back, Sally was standing with my

dad. "Hershel seems really nice," said Sally.

"He is," I said. "He's like my best friend out here."

"He's kind of strange, huh?" Sally asked.

"Yeah, that's Hershel."

"Funny too," said Sally. "And I think he likes you."

"What makes you say that?"

"It's just a feeling I get." Sally shrugged her shoulders. "Could be nothing." Sally looked at all the other people on the beach. "Where's this Jake guy that you like?"

"I told you, I don't like him anymore. He has a girlfriend and she's a jerk. I think he's a jerk too."

"Point him out anyway?"

I saw Jake in a crowd of boys from my class. He was talking with his hands like he always did. "He's that one over there . . . in the orange and green shorts."

Sally looked at Jake. "Wow, he *is* cute. But I think Hershel's cuter."

"What are you talking about?" I asked.

"I think Hershel's cuter. I just do," said Sally.

I found Portia in the crowd and pointed her out to Sally as well. Sally made a circle with her left hand then clapped three times.

"What was that?" I asked.

"I just cursed her," said Sally. "I saw this thing on television about witches. That's how they curse people."

"Thanks, I guess." I shook my head at her.

"No problem."

We hung around on the beach waiting for my turn to compete. There were worse places to be nervous. It was turning into a gorgeous day, even at seven in the morning.

The Super Wave Junior Championship was set up by boy and girl age groups. All the boys in the same age group would compete against each other. The same thing applied for the girls. The sixteen-year-olds went first. Some of the rides were awesome, and the tricks were killer. One girl did a 360, turning her entire board around in a wave. It was incredible.

"Can you do that?" Sally asked me.

"Not yet," I said. "A few weeks ago, I couldn't even get up on the board."

"Well, you could do that on a snowboard. I've seen it. I bet you could surf circles around that girl."

Sally was trying to build me up, but I really wasn't that good yet. "Seriously, I'm still learning, Sally. Surfing and snowboarding are totally different," I said.

We watched more of the competition. Finally, it was the twelve-year-old boys' turn. We cheered Hershel on. He wasn't the most graceful surfer in the world, but he was fearless. Any wave that was near him, he would take. He rode more waves than anyone else in the time he was out there. I was yelling for Hershel louder than anyone else.

There was this kid from another school who was by far the best out there. This guy was amazing. He reminded me of Mrs. Blossom.

I spotted Portia down the beach with a few of her friends. I noticed a few of them point to the amazing surfer and smile. Portia turned around and snapped something at them. They immediately stopped pointing and smiling.

When the boys' heat was over, it was my group's turn. Mrs. Blossom ran up to wish us all luck. She gave me a hug. "Good luck out there, Cece, and no matter what happens . . ."

"I know." She didn't need to finish her sentence. "I'm just going to enjoy the ocean."

There were about twenty girls or so in my age group. We were standing by the shore, waiting to start. We had fifteen minutes in our heat. The judges would score our best two rides. A judges voice rang out over the loudspeaker: "Twelve year old girls will start in five, four, three . . ."

I took a deep breath and jumped up and down on the sand.

". . . two, one, go!"

We took off paddling. We were all spread out, hoping that our positions would be perfect for a wave. I spotted a nice one forming. I quickly turned around and started to paddle as hard as I could. I just barely missed it. I felt it go under me. "Okay, Cece, get the next one," I whispered to myself.

I paddled back out again. Pretty soon another wave was coming my way. I turned around and paddled hard, digging my arms deep. My arms started to burn, but I kept going. The wave came under me, and my board stayed with it. I caught the wave and stood up on it. As soon as I was up on my feet, though, I lost my balance. I fell over into the water.

The wave crashed over me, knocking me around under water. My board tugged on my leg as it was pulled to the shore. I came up to the surface and swam to my board.

"You got a little too excited there," I said to myself. "You can do this."

I looked up and saw Portia riding a wave. I paddled back out.

"Ten minutes remain," shouted the man on the loudspeaker.

In the next five minutes, I caught two more waves. They weren't very long rides. Still, I stood up and was able to make a few turns on the board. I would say I was somewhere right in the middle of the pack of girls. I wasn't the best, but I certainly wasn't the worst either.

"Five minutes remain."

I caught the next wave for my longest ride of the day so far. The problem was, it took me all the way to the shore. This meant that I had a long way to paddle back out. It also meant that I probably only had one ride left. I paddled as hard as I could to get out past the break.

When I got there, I barely had a chance to catch my breath. A huge, beautiful wave was headed right towards me. I was in the perfect spot to catch the biggest wave I had ever seen. I turned around as fast as I could, and started paddling. The problem was that when I turned, I noticed Portia next to me. She was trying to catch the same perfect wave. We both paddled as the wave formed behind us.

"Get off my wave, Wyoming."

"No," I said to Portia. "It's my wave too."

The wave came closer as we paddled next to each other.

I dug my arms deeper. I pulled slightly ahead of Portia. I kept paddling as hard as I could. I was about half-a-board's length in front of her when the wave arrived. We both popped up at the same time. Only I was in the right spot. I stood all the way up, just as Portia wiped out behind me.

I was going so fast that I was a little scared at first. That fear quickly turned into a deep concentration. Everything seemed to disappear around me. It was like I was alone in the wave. For those few seconds, time slowed down to a stop. I could hear my surfboard's fin slicing through the water. I could feel the wave underneath my board. Every movement I made was in sync with the wave. We were one. I knew exactly what the wave was going to do. I had never felt more alive.

I carved beautiful Cs, just like my name. Cece was here. Cece was here.

For that one ride, I was the best surfer in the competition. I rode that wave like I had been surfing my entire life. I stayed on longer than any ride I've ever taken. And when the wave peeked, I did an awesome carve. I shot up the wave and then landed perfectly. It was great. "Woohoo!" I shouted.

When the wave reached the shore, I remembered that I was at a competition. The people on the beach applauded me for my ride. I jumped off my board. I knew I hadn't won, but I hadn't embarrassed myself either. I was definitely a legit surfer.

Oscar was pretty easy to spot in the crowd. He was the only standard poodle at the Super Wave Championship. Sally was holding his leash, cheering and jumping up and down like a crazy person. Hershel was standing next to Sally going nuts. My dad was going nuts too. This time, he was dressed in shorts and a t-shirt. He left his gorilla costume at home. My face hurt I was smiling so much.

I turned around and saw Portia swimming back to shore. "Guess it was my wave after all," I called to her.

I noticed Jake walking towards me. At first I thought he was coming to help Portia, but he came right up to me. "Wow, Cece. That was an incredible ride. You really nailed that carve. I had no idea you were so good."

"Thanks." I just looked at him.

Jake stood there in front of me smiling. "Can I help you bring in your board?" If Jake had asked me that a few months ago, I would have been thrilled.

I looked over at Hershel standing with Sally and Oscar. Then I looked at Portia dragging herself out of the water. "No thanks," I said. "But it looks like Portia could use a little help."

I walked over to meet my friends and my dad.

"Oh, Cece, I am so proud of you. You surfed so beautifully out there. You're really good!" Dad looked shocked by my surfing skills.

"Thank you," I said, giving him a hug.

Sally squealed with delight and joined us, "You are awesome, girl!"

Oscar licked my hand.

When I let go of my father and Sally, I noticed Hershel. "Excellent riding, Cece," he said.

I turned around to face him. "I couldn't have done this without your help, you know." The sight of him standing there made me realize that Sally was right. Hershel was really cute. And I did something that I totally didn't expect. I gave him a kiss right on his lips, in front of everyone.

Hershel smiled at me. "Excellent indeed," he said.

CHAPTER TWENTY

NIGHT SWIMMING

That night, I walked up to the trophy shelf on my bookcase. In my hand, I held the ribbon from today. It read: Super Wave Championship—Twelve-Year-Old Girls—Fourth Place. I opened my drawer with the Three Special Things. Then I placed the ribbon next to the picture of my parents. I was going to have to rename this stuff My Four Special Things.

Oscar put his paws on my feet and licked my right ankle.

"Hey, boy, go wake Sally up." I told him while putting him on the bed. He walked over to Sally and started licking her face.

Five minutes later she was awake and we were both in our bathing suits. The three of us ran downstairs to take a late night swim. Even at midnight, it was fun just being in the water.

TEST YOURSELF...ARE YOU A PROFESSIONAL READER?

Chapter 1: Big Chill

What is the "Big Chill?" Why did Cece feel so comfortable at the top of the "Big Chill?"

What sight caused Cece to move off-line and wipe out during the last heat?

Who was inside the gorilla suit?

ESSAY

In Chapter 1, we are introduced to Cece. We learn that she loves to snowboard and about her relationship with her father. Now, write an introduction about yourself. Include details about where you're from, your family, your hobbies...etc.).

Chapter 2: Growing up Chili

Why didn't Cece want people outside of Rockville to read the article that featured Rockville Mountain?

Why do most kids think Cece is lucky that Mad Marty is her father?

Who are Cece's two best friends?

ESSAY

In this chapter, Cece begins to talk about what profession she would eventually like to pursue. What are some goals of your own that you're aiming to achieve in the years ahead? Have you picked out a possible profession yet?

Chapter 3: The Phone Call and Chapter 4: Cece and Sally

How did Cece feel about the possibility of moving to Los Angeles?

Where do Sally and Cece meet when they need to talk about important stuff?

What is Big Bison? What did Cece think about her snowboarding future after she called Big Bison?

ESSAY

In these chapters, it becomes clear that Cece and her dad are going to move to Los Angeles. Have you ever moved before? If so, describe your feelings when you had to relocate. If you've never moved, what is one place where you'd like to move? Explain how moving might affect you.

Chapter 5: The Rearview Mirror and Chapter 6: Entering Los Angeles

What are Cece's Three Special Things?

What was in Cece's 'Just in Case' box? Why did she call that box her 'Just in Case' box?

What was Sally's "going-away" present for Cece?

ESSAY

Cece takes one last ride on Rockville Mountain before she leaves town. Again, her obvious love of snowboarding is displayed. Detail a sport or hobby that you enjoy. Why do you like this particular sport/hobby?

Chapter 7: New School Disaster and Chapter 8: The Magician

Why did Cece immediately feel comfortable with Mrs. Blossom?

How did Cece know Hershel's name before he even said a word to her?

Who followed Cece into the girls' bathroom when she was upset? How did this person know exactly how Cece was feeling?

ESSAY

From these chapters, we learn that Cece has a favorite teacher, Mrs. Blossom. Who is your favorite teacher or coach? Explain why this person is your favorite teacher or coach. What have you learned from him/her?

Chapter 9: The Big Blue Ocean and Chapter 10: Surf's Up

Where did Cece's dad take her after she had a bad day at school?

What good news did Mrs. Blossom have for Cece when she saw her at the beach?

What does Hershel call robotic monkeys?

ESSAY

Portia has become a pain in Cece's side with her constant harassment. Why do you think that Portia goes out of her way to make Cece feel unwelcome? Explain.

Chapter 11: Collision Course and Chapter 12: Lost

Why was Hershel laughing when Cece told him that her foam board might be broken?

Why didn't Cece tell her mom the truth about her time in Los Angeles?

What did Cece think of the fake snow at Big Bison?

ESSAY

In Chapter 12, Cece is disappointed with the snowboarding condi tions at Big Bison. Write about a time in your life when you had high expectations, but ended up being disappointed. Or, write about a time when someone or something exceeded your expectations.

Chapter 13: Bad to Worse and Chapter 14: Waking Up

Why was Cece paranoid when her dad called her "Cece" instead of "Chili?"

Why did Cece feel like she was "sleepwalking" through life?

When does Cece "wake up" in Chapter 14?

ESSAY

Cece has had some unfortunate occurrences in her life up to this point. Yet, in Chapter 14, she "decided to stop letting things that I couldn't control make me sad." What does she mean by this? How could you use Cece's words in your life?

Chapter 15: Standing Up and Chapter 16: Just Do It

What animal did Cece actually see when she thought that sharks were swimming around her?

What good news did Hershel share with Cece during lunch?

What does Cece discover about the best way to deal with bullies?

ESSAY

In Chapter 15, Cece overcomes a fear of hers by "standing up" and confronting Portia. How did Portia react to Cece's tough response? Detail an instance in your life when you had to deal with a bully or simply overcome a fear.

Chapter 17: Training and Chapter 18: Surfer

According to Hershel, why is he always busy with various experiments?

When did Cece become "officially hooked" to the sport of surfing?

What did Cece eventually realize about Jake?

ESSAY

In these chapters, the fact that Hershel believes in Cece and her abilities is obvious. In turn, Cece begins to believe in herself. Why is it so important to believe in yourself? Do you believe in yourself? Explain.

Chapter 19: The Ride and Chapter 20: Night Swimming

What did Sally think about Cece's home in Los Angeles?

How did Sally "curse" Portia? How did Sally learn this technique?

What item became Cece's Fourth Special Thing?

ESSAY

Congratulations! You have completed another Scobre Press book! After joining Cece on her journey, detail what you learned from her life and experiences. How are you going to use Cece's story to help you achieve your dreams? What did Cece teach you about trying new activities that you aren't necessarily skilled in?